Amazing Grace

Also by Robert Drake

Fiction
The Single Heart
The Burning Bush
Survivors and Others

Criticism
Flannery O'Connor
(Contemporary Writers in Christian Perspective)

Memoir
The Home Place: A Memory and a Celebration

Amazing Grace

Twenty-fifth

Anniversary Edition

Robert Drake

MERCER UNIVERSITY PRESS

ISBN 0-86554-364-X [casebound]
ISBN 0-86554-372-0 [perfectbound]

Amazing Grace
Twenty-fifth Anniversary Edition
Copyright © 1990
Mercer University Press
Macon, Georgia 31207
All rights reserved
See acknowledgments on page xv
Printed in the United States of America

The paper used in this publication meets the
minimum requirements of American National
Standard for Information Sciences—
Permanence of Paper for Printed Library Materials,
∞   ANSI Z39.48-1984.

Library of Congress Cataloging-in-Publication Data

Drake, Robert, 1930–
Amazing grace / Robert Drake.—25th anniv. ed.
xxiv + 116pp. 15 × 23cm. 6 × 9in.
ISBN 0-86554-364-X (alk. paper)
ISBN 0-86554-372-0 (pbk. : alk. paper)
1. Tennessee, West—fiction. I. Title.
PS3554.R237A8   1990   89-49335
813'.54—dc20   CIP

Contents

Raising Ebenezers

A Foreword

After one of many engagements when the Lord helped him and the Israelites to chase away the Philistines, the prophet Samuel marked the happy occasion by erecting a stone pillar—a kind of permanent thank offering. Once he raised his Ebenezer, even the prophet made little enough of the episode; but it was enough for one Robert Robinson, a late eighteenth-century versifier, to refer to it (with no explanation) in "Come, Thou Fount of Every Blessing" (1758). Most congregations today never get to raise their Ebenezers. Presumably on the theory that we have no business singing anything that is not instantly clear, we are now conformed to this world by singing "alt."—the quiet little rubric favored by so many modern hymnologists—in which "Here I'll raise mine Ebenezer" becomes "Here I find my greatest treasure." The two of course are not the same, even if the newer line *is* a fine sentiment. In the original, the beneficiary memorializes his gratitude; in the altered state he secularizes the gift of divine help with a metaphor of ownership. I prefer the old kind of praise, and I am happy to find that the author of *Amazing Grace* does, too.

Though Robert Drake as youthful narrator never quite discovers what the old hymn means "about raising your Ebenezer," we may be quite certain that Robert Drake as author knows all about it. *Amazing Grace* is *his* Ebenezer: a tangible and permanent thank offering that commemorates his own grace-filled passage from boyhood to adulthood in a little West Tennessee town.

But it is not place--that overvalued component in Southern fiction—that makes *Amazing Grace* worth our pleasure. These are stories whose strengths are nuance and color and characterization; what makes them memorable is a finely traced depiction of unremarkable people going about doing what unremarkable people do. Uncle John, the picture-taking Methodist preacher; Herbert Fisher, the genial ne'er-do-well; Mrs. Higgins, the bighearted widow with a terrible temper; Cousin Rosa Moss, the schoolteacher who wastes little breath over the telephone; and others supply the texture of ordinary life in a town still linked in spirit and memory to modest country privilege.

Several of the stories announce by their titles the dominant thread of evangelical Protestantism in that texture of life in the old rural towns of the South. "The Fountain Filled with Blood," "The Bridegroom Cometh," "By Thy Good Pleasure," and of course the title story all allude to and generously quote from familiar hymn texts, which by their available immediacy only a generation ago rivaled even the King James Bible as touchstones for behavior, ratified every Sunday for application during the week. As the youthful narrating voice makes clear, calling yourself a wretch or a worm in the singing of hymns did not require a long face. It is not so much the pieties of religious certitude that nourish the spirit of Drake's people but a buoyancy of affirmation enacted in tireless repetition—affirmation that love divine (all loves excelling!) very particularly has a human dimension that includes little kooks, old crocks, and eccentric neighbors as well as parents, uncles, aunts, and cousins.

The religious thread knits together the various strands of *Amazing Grace* because it knits together the effective life of the community that Drake depicts, an ambience of generosity rather than restriction. A kind of testy tolerance, while it pervades the familial and communal life of Woodville, always gets its severest testing by general human behavior, not at the spectacle of marital misconduct (as in "Mr. Andrew and the Big Cedar Tree") but in the violation of ordinary common sense (as in "Mrs. Higgins's Heart," in which "Mamma" Drake comments on the overrated reputation of

a local cake-baker, "You can't make a cake out of water and margarine and expect it to stand up").

Amazing Grace was the author's first book, but by the time I read
it (not in 1965 but in the 1980 Eerdmans edition), I had already from
periodical publication become exposed to Drake's Woodville and
its richly, if sparsely, populated environs and their kinetic talkers
and doers. Both the country town and its inhabitants, I told myself, were clearly only semifictional. This feeling I suspect is a felt
thing for most readers familiar with modern Southern literature
generally, but in this instance it was indirectly confirmed by the
author himself in *The Home Place* (Memphis State University Press,
1980). In this vivid series of pieces whose subject is the Drake family, its author readily admits that Woodville is his hometown, Ripley, Tennessee—and, further, that his study is not strictly history
("I have changed some names, dates, and details of the action to
give better shape to the picture"). It was at this point that I turned
to *Amazing Grace*, in which the urgencies of autobiographical truth
clearly required only the minimal demands of fictional art to re-
lease them. Most memoirs, truth to tell, stretch and shape and al-
ter the reality that grounds them, but not many writers of memoirs
feel obliged to admit that fact. Of course *The Home Place* is molded
by the gifts of imagination; through *Amazing Grace* and subsequent
pieces Ripley by 1980 had already been transformed into Woodville. It is almost as if, having already committed himself to light
fictionalizing of the recent past in his *stories*, Drake felt compelled
to continue the practice in a book of *memoirs*. (Generic purists will
complain: *The Home Place*, because it is about the author's family,
not the author, can scarcely be called *memoirs*; yet it is assuredly at
least the *work* of a memoirist.) If as an artist Drake wanted to lend
"something of a rounded whole" to *The Home Place*, it is also as an
artist that he disallows the importunings of fiction to distort its
"essential historical truth."

Rereading the stories in *Amazing Grace* suggests to me that the
conscientiousness that governed Drake's historical account gov-
erns his fictional accounts as well. The narrating voice we hear so
distinctly in *Survivors and Others* (Mercer University Press, 1987) is
older, more sophisticated, more relentless in ferreting out the all-
too-human antics of Woodville people than the boyish-adolescent
teller of *Amazing Grace*; but the same curiosity, the same observant

eye and open ear, the same rich appreciation for the human comedy in all its mutations were present in full measure in Drake's first book. The diverse characters, we feel, are not just figures summoned from scratch by the needs of a fictionist; they must have had their first lives in the context of actual experience. Miss Jo-Ellen Bates, Aunt Janie, Mrs. Edney, Miss Eunice Grace Patterson, the Moss sisters, and all the rest owe their resurrected life to a writer who demands of his art both "a rounded whole" and "essential historical truth." And no one who reads "Amazing Grace" and "By Thy Good Pleasure" can doubt that "Daddy" Drake is father as well as character, a serviceable figure in a story certainly, but whose prior service must have been in the greater one of personal history.

The classicist John Andrew Rice, the principal founder of Black Mountain College, wrote in his fragmentary memoirs that he was a "born Southerner," the experience of which meant that ideas and things "induced a yawn," but "let a name be mentioned, my tribe was off." Along with other small children growing up in the South, he listened to and learned from "words, tone, gesture," and from his adult perspective concluded, "What we learned was that, of all the world had to offer, people were the most interesting." Robert Drake would say amen to that. As we know, his little book of 1965 did not exhaust his collection of interesting people— *Survivors and Others* surpassed it in range, depth, and sheer number of portraits—but, like the prophet's raising of the stone of help for the faithful to note, it still compels our regard. *Amazing Grace* is Drake's Ebenezer, but it is our treasure.

—*James H. Justus*

Preface

to the Twenty-Fifth

Anniversary Edition

It's hard for me to realize that *Amazing Grace* is twenty-five years old and that even I myself am a quarter-century older than I was when it first appeared. Many people have told me that it was their favorite of all my books; and of course it was my first "child" and, in some ways, is still for me the most intimate and personal of them all. For one thing, I use my own name for that of the narrator; and of course many of the events narrated draw heavily on those of my own life. But I think it would be a mistake to regard the book as thinly disguised autobiography because of course imagination, more than memory, is really dominant there. It's my concern in the stories to make sense out of my life and my world, not on a one-to-one basis, the way of history, but in a more formal way, the way of art.

What is it like to grow up where I did and when I did—in a small West Tennessee town in the thirties and forties? What is it like to become conscious of your own context the more you learn about others—and about the greatest context of all, which is the big wide world itself? What is it like, finally, to discover the self? That's what I think the stories are about, and perhaps that's what makes them true for people who never saw—or heard of—West Tennessee. There's a chronological "clothes line" to hang them on too. So there is a progressive narrative from start to finish. But again, I don't think this necessarily makes the book either autobiography or memoir. I'll still settle for the shape and form of fiction, whether it's a collection of stories or something even approaching the novel.

And I never meant to write any of it. Trained to be a teacher and a scholar, I had never given a thought to writing fiction until one of my senior colleagues in my first teaching job suggested it to me and another of them, the late Austin Warren, began reading my first attempts and giving me encouragement—something he never stopped doing either until the day of his death thirty years later. But what really kept me going during those first years, when the big brown envelopes I used for submitting my work kept coming back with considerable regularity, was the conviction that well, I was a teacher by trade and, if nothing else, perhaps trying to write fiction would teach me more about how it worked and thereby help me to teach it more effectively. And truly, I believe it did.

But meanwhile the stories kept piling up, and I really at that point had no idea where they were going. (I think now of my father, who would never order soup in a restaurant: he said they didn't *make* soup there, they just *accumulated* it!) But gradually there came to me some idea of what I was trying to do: I wanted to make sense of my life and what I had learned about the world, what I had survived and lived to tell—and where, you might say, I had come out at. (That was a game my father and I played, when as a boy I rode all over the county with him, when he went out on business, over all sorts of back roads and byways. And he would try me out, test me on the local geography by asking me to tell him where we would "come out at" on the main highways when he had concluded his errands in the country and started on back to town. And thus I would prove—or not prove—my knowledge of my world and perhaps also myself.)

And it all took seven years—a term of trial perhaps not unlike some of those imposed in the Bible. Meanwhile some of the stories had begun appearing in periodicals, and I had even recorded some of them for broadcast by the B.B.C. in London. But only when I met Flannery O'Connor, whose work I greatly admired, in 1963 did the possibility of a whole book really seem not merely dreaming. Because she referred me to her agent in New York, Elizabeth McKee; and the next year—ironically, shortly after Flannery's untimely death—Elizabeth was able to place the manuscript with John Marion, an editor at Chilton Books in Philadelphia. And it was they who brought out the book in 1965—and without changing a word either.

Only one change was made in the original manuscript, and I made that one myself. After the book had gone into production I got unhappy about one of the stories included and sent John a special delivery, air mail letter (I was too scared to phone!) asking him to withdraw that story and insert another piece I was sending him in its place. And now I almost tremble to think of my presumption. But John was obliging, and it all seemed finally a happy decision because the inserted piece, "The Store," which I asked him to use as a sort of prologue to the volume, turned out to be the one piece that prompted the most comment from readers all over the country. And it's of course not fiction but absolutely fact: a memoir of Drake Brothers, the hardware and grocery store owned and operated by my father and my uncle, a very real institution in Ripley, Tennessee, and, along with the town and the Methodist Church, the beginning of everything there is to know about me and my world.

Yes, many of the readers who wrote me had known such a store—or thought they had. It wasn't exactly a "general" store but mainly one set up to furnish farmers and their tenants with the supplies for making a cotton crop; but it was "general" in all the important ways in the sense that it was a center for community life and news. And its rhythm both daily and seasonal was almost something like the heartbeat of the town and the county itself. You might even say that it was a microcosm of that time and place. And that's what the readers who wrote me seemed to feel, along with their persuasion that in the book I hadn't just been recollecting my own particular history but writing about them all. Indeed, I know now, I had been writing fiction.

And the book got some attention in the press and, for a book of its sort, sold well: the hardcover first edition sold out its printing of 5,000 copies. Then in 1980 it was brought out in paperback by the William B. Eerdmans Publishing Company of Grand Rapids, and that edition sold respectably too. But it's been out of print for nearly ten years now, and I'm of course very happy that it will once more be available for readers—and especially in this handsome anniversary edition. And new generations will have a chance to become acquainted with me and my world. Some things about that world of some fifty years ago will now seem dated, even perhaps distressing to readers who don't remember the time of segregation and covert or even open racism. But like Conrad, I've never felt the writer had any duty other than telling the truth; and for me that means warts and all, the way it really is. But of course I don't see myself as writing *news*, at least in the sense of headlines; and I'm certainly not trying to convert anybody to anything, whether religion or social program. I'm just trying to write about *folks* and the main story there always is to tell about them—what Faulkner called the human heart in conflict with itself. And I've tried to do it from my own peculiar vantage point, my own eye on the world, which of course is finally the only thing any writer ever has to offer us—his own vision.

Since *Amazing Grace* I've gone on to write three more books of stories and also a book about my father's family—a sort of cultural memoir, I think. And I've done my time, paid my professional dues with over a hundred essays and reviews in the academic and other journals. Yes, though I still think of myself mainly as a teacher, I'm a "productive" scholar and critic as well as a "writer." Yet I should like to think that these two sides of my life are not contradictory but complementary. In any case, they're perhaps what my life has added up to, where it has come out at—as of now at any rate. But I think, in more ways than one, that this book started it all, in what it taught me about my craft, in what it taught me about myself. But to explain *that* I can only fall back on the concluding lines of the first stanza in the old hymn, the first one I ever learned, which still speak for me better than I ever can myself: "I once was lost, but now am found, / Was blind, but now I see."

I am indebted to the Hodges Better English Fund at the University of Tennessee, Knoxville, which assisted publication of this edition; to Professor James H. Justus of Indiana University for kind words and kind deeds on more than one occasion; and to Mr. Edd Rowell of the Mercer University Press, who believed in this venture from the very beginning.

—R.D.

Acknowledgments

"Brother Haynes and the Nine-Year-Old Evangelist" appeared originally in a slightly different version as "The Nine-Year-Old Evangelist" in the *Michigan Alumnus Quarterly Review* (1957), now the *Michigan Quarterly Review*, and is reprinted by permission.

"Daddy and the Bull Named Herbert" and "Uncle John and the Trail of the Years" appeared originally in the *Arizona Quarterly* (1960 and 1961 respectively), and are reprinted by permission.

"Easy Steps for Little Feet," "Amazing Grace," and "The Fountain Filled with Blood" appeared originally in *The Christian Century* (1960, 1961, 1963 respectively), and are reprinted by permission.

"By Thy Good Pleasure" appeared originally in the *Christian Herald* (1964) and is reprinted by permission.

"The Summer of the Window-Peeper," "Mr. Andrew and the Big Cedar Tree," "Brother Haynes and the Nine-Year-Old Evangelist," and "Mr. Marcus and the Overhead Bridge" were all recorded by the author in London for broadcast on a B.B.C. Home Service feature program called "Tonight's Short Story," on which authors read from their own works.

Most of the older photographs in the Photo Album are the work of the Rev. W. L. Drake.

The first edition of *Amazing Grace* was published in 1965 by Chilton Books, Chilton Company, Philadelphia and New York, and was published simultaneously by Ambassador Books, Ltd., Toronto. A paperback reprint was published in 1980 by William B. Eerdmans Publishing Co., Grand Rapids. For this twenty-fifth anniversary edition, the text was completely redesigned and an anniversary preface and foreword were added; otherwise the text is essentially that of the first edition.

Amazing grace! how sweet the sound,
That saved a wretch like me!
I once was lost, but now am found,
Was blind, but now I see.

—John Newton (1725–1807)

(Originally the first stanza of a six-stanza hymn entitled "Faith's Review and Expectation" that first appeared in William Cowper and Newton's *Olney Hymns,* 1779.)

A Photo Album

The house on Jefferson Street in Ripley, Tennessee, where I was born and grew up.

Drake Brothers, soon after it was opened for business in 1921. My father and my uncle are, respectively, second and fifth from the left.

I was about six years old when this was taken on our front steps.

My grandfather—Pa Drake—flanked by two other veterans, en route to a Confederate reunion. The black man had accompanied his master to the war as a body servant.

One of Uncle Lewis's group pictures of a Drake Christmas dinner, this one was made around 1938 at Uncle Walter's house in Henning. Since the five Drake brothers were extremely fond of one another and, after Uncle Lewis retired from the ministry, all lived in Lauderdale County, we naturally had five Christmas dinners every year.

My parents and I, taken about the time I went off to graduate school at Yale in 1953.

The five Drake brothers photographed after a Christmas dinner, in the late forties—here posed in order of age, oldest to youngest, from right to left: Lewis; Walter; George; my father, Robert; and Sanford.

The brothers at another Christmas dinner, around 1950, photographed on the front steps of our house. You can tell that they're all just about to burst into laughter—something they were always inclined to do when things got too solemn.

A former student of mine, Jeanne Holloway-Ridley, made this photograph when I was presiding over an informal session during Eudora Welty's visit to the University of Tennessee, Knoxville, in 1980.

1

The Store

When I was a little boy growing up in West Tennessee, a great part of my life was centered in my father and uncle's place of business, known to the public as Drake Brothers but to us simply as "the store." It was a type of business establishment no longer often seen, even in small Southern farming communities such as the one where I grew up; and even in my childhood it was becoming something of an anomaly.

It is best described as a combination hardware and staple grocery store (*not* a "general" store), with several subsidiary enterprises operating on the fringe—upstairs and in the back. But the primary combination was that of hardware and staple (as distinguished from "fancy" or fresh) groceries, a conjunction scrupulously observed in the almost equal division of the main body of the store between them. On one's right as he entered the long "shotgun" building opening immediately off the courthouse square was the hardware "side"; on the left, the staple groceries. And between them, stretching all the way to the back door, which opened onto an alley, was a sort of neutral zone in the form of a fairly wide, clear aisle, which served as the principal artery of the store's circulation—the broad highway of commerce and personal encounter. The store's "livery," in which most of its fixtures were painted, was the traditional "hardware colors" of black and orange; its smells, varied, rich, and strange.

To a small boy, of course, the hardware side was the more interesting, with, first, its cases of rifles and shotguns, carefully stood on end and gleaming in burnished and, I had been warned, mortal beauty. After that fascination came the long, high glass counter displaying all sorts of implements for cutting and, again fear-somely, mutilation: shining knives—pocket and butcher--and scis-sors for every conceivable domestic purpose. On top of this counter were two additional sources of wonderment: a low, cylindrical, metallic case containing sewing machine needles and bobbins, the correct size and shape located by spinning a dial on top of the cyl-inder *before* opening the slot found there for their extraction, and a small glass case containing all the paraphernalia of shaving—straight and safety razors, strops, brushes, blades, and soap.

Proceeding down the hardware side, one next encountered the long, low Coca-Cola box in which not only that beverage but other, taller drinks (better known as "belly-washers"—and much pre-ferred by the Negroes) were kept chilled by a large block of ice bought the first thing every morning at the city ice plant over by the fire station. Here, for most of the white customers, was the sto-re's heart, where they might, with friends, idle away an hour in relaxed and genial conversation of weather, crops, men, and things. Here were old tales retold, present speculations mooted, and future undertakings proclaimed. And it was here, finally, that my father, the store's animating spirit and presiding genius, who was literally all over the place from morning till night, *seemed* most generally to be found, the boldest speculator and grandest remem-berer of them all.

Next on the side after the Coca-Cola box was the telephone, sit-ting on a small, high desk and freely and very publicly used by owners, employees, customers, and what my father rather per-emptorily dismissed as just plain "boosters" (loafers) alike. Then there were several counters of kitchen utensils and a display case of garden seeds before one came to the foot of the staircase, which led up past great coils of rope, on turntables for easy dispensing, to the second story, used largely for storage purposes but also con-taining such allurements as a tank for minnows which had been created, quite simply and effectively, by sawing in two a great oil drum laid lengthwise. (I was told that minnows were delicate crea-tures and therefore cautioned not to "play with" them with the various nets. I *was* allowed to feed them from time to time.)

Under the staircase were bins for nuts, bolts, nails, and screws. And then finally at the very back, and in the corner, still on the hardware side, was the office. Certainly no larger than eight feet by ten in dimensions, it was bounded on the outside by two waist-high counters, on the inside by the walls themselves. And it was here that my uncle was to be found a great deal of the time, sitting on a towering high stool, carefully posting the books and making out statements and settling the accounts of such customers as had come in to pay. Also in the office was a desk on which stood a rather Gothic-looking Underwood typewriter of ancient design and above which hung a picture of Woodrow Wilson ("Our Twenty-eighth President"), who, along with William Jennings Bryan, was one of my father's modern heroes. And under the counters there were a small safe, a number of shelves containing booklike letter files, and the catalogues for the current and all previous years from the great hardware wholesale houses: Orgill Brothers (Memphis), Belknap (Louisville), and, grandest of all because thickest and from farthest away, Shapleigh (St. Louis).

Behind all the counters on the hardware side there were, of course, shelves and drawers containing tools, implements, and parts: plow points, trace chains, monkey wrenches, and other wonders. And there were, somewhere near the stairs, I believe, an assortment of horse collars hanging on pegs in the wall and a re-volving stand of murderous-looking axes stood upside down on their heads.

The lighter, domestic aspect of the store lay across the aisle on the side of the staple groceries. It began just inside the front door with the glass candy showcase, which, when I was very little and my father was telling me stories at bedtime, he would propose to fill with red candy for the delight of all such little boys as came in the store because it was a well-known fact that all little boys loved red candy better than anything else in the *whole united world.* As a rule, though, the candy case contained an assortment of the usual candy bars and the most tempting varieties of gum drops, pep-permint sticks, and "hard" candies, the latter usually twisted into tortured baroque shapes and invariably stuck together so that one inevitably, on reaching in for a small piece when the eye of au-thority was turned, was forced to take a much larger piece than he "meant" to. On top of the candy counter there was a round metal box containing sugared, grated coconut, very delicious to the clan-destine taste but scorned by my mother, who much preferred *fresh* coconut, along with its milk, for her memorable coconut cakes.

Next after the candy counter on the grocery side was a small counter on which stood the cash register and cigar case. (Cigarettes, snuff, and chewing tobacco were found on shelves behind it.) And then came a very long counter, used largely for wrapping and packaging, at whose nearer end was a stand for great rolls of brown paper in various widths and a big spool of string, beneath which, incidentally, lived a family of most interesting bugs ("string bugs," I called them) which I used periodically to attack, never successfully, with the Flit. At the farther end of the counter were scales and a revolving cheese stand with cutting lever, which always held a hoop of "nigger" or "rat" cheese with a fascinating design of the state of Wisconsin stamped on it in purple ink. A very large open box of crackers usually stood beside it: a purchase of "a dime's worth of cheese and crackers" was not uncommon and thus easily arranged. Behind this long counter were shelves for canned goods and bins for such staples as bulk coffee, sugar, and rice, where a great deal of quiet enjoyment for a small boy was to be found, until the management intervened, in mixing the various staples so as to observe the interesting effects produced by their contrasting colors and textures.

Beyond the long counter toward the back of the store there were bins of citrus fruits, apples, potatoes, and onions, and then, on a raised platform, tall columns of flour sacks, both regular and self-rising. (Wonderful name that latter variety! It had all sorts of Easter connotations in my mind.)

Then came the stove, eight feet tall and, at its middle, nearly three feet in diameter, around which clustered the Negroes, gossiping, nursing their babies (sometimes even changing a diaper!), or, in winter, just sitting quietly on a nail-keg, basking happily in the radiant tropical heat. For *them*, the *stove* was the heart of the store, and they continued to sit there even in the summertime when it was fireless and cold. I suspect now that the stove area was tacitly understood to be their Jim Crow province, but I think also that the stove was important to them in itself. I know that my father firmly believed that no Negro had any liking for central heating: he wanted to be where he could *sweat* comfortably and profusely. And I myself feel that in some way the stove became for them what it never was for the whites: a source of more than elemental heat—perhaps a symbol, though dimly perceived, of life and vitality itself, a steady white core of warmth and light blessing and dispelling a dark, pervasive chill. In drawing near it so regularly and ceremonially they somehow warmed and renewed their souls as well as their bodies.

Beyond the stove, at the very back of the grocery side, was the "cotton office"—a high table where my uncle examined and graded cotton samples and generally carried on the business of what was known to the bank as the store's "cotton account." Sometimes he bought for the store itself; sometimes he acted as an agent for a big Memphis firm. But always he moved there in a great world of mysterious intangibles such as "middling" and "strict-low-middling," of which the white rolls of sample cotton were but the mundane and inadequate signs. And to hear him talk, as he often did there, of *hundreds* of bales and *thousands* of dollars and speak familiarly not only of Memphis but also of *New Orleans* and *New York* gave to the enterprise a grand dimension which carried one in imagination far beyond the store and the town to the great world of affairs and the ends of the earth itself.

The store's pulse corresponded almost exactly to that of the farming community which it served. Fall was the busiest season, and Saturday the busiest day. But even then the pace was not accelerated, only intensified: time was never a rationed commodity for either customers or clerks. Significantly, there was no clock in the main body of the store. There *was* an impressive rococo wall clock, the gift of a spice and condiments firm, in one of the front display windows; but it could be seen from within only by means of a special effort. And its muffled ticking rarely obtruded on the consciousness. Christmas then seemed not so much a rush season in itself as the natural and logical climax of the busy harvesttime. And afterwards there was always the "slow" period when accounts were settled (or not), inventory taken, and profits and losses figured, until credit "opened" on the first of March and the store's customers could begin "buying" against the next fall's crop. And the cycle would begin once more. Through it, sooner or later, passed most of the people of the town and the county, whether to buy, "visit" with one another over a Coca-Cola, or perhaps watch or join in the checker game which ran almost without interruption upstairs. And no matter what the time or the season, the store was rarely quiet, often crowded, and always alive.

The store and my father are both gone now; and only my uncle, now a banker, remains as a link for me with that time and place.* The community which the store was designed to serve and the agricultural tradition out of which it grew have changed much and doubtless will change more. Indeed, there seems to be little place for such enterprises there today: my home town can boast of supermarkets and chain specialty stores along with the best of them, and soy beans and stock farming bring in more money for some people than cotton. I myself no longer live there; but whenever I return to visit my uncle, I still see many people, white and black—some old friends, others barely acquaintances, who tell me how much they miss both my father and the store and assure me of how warm a place they both held in their lives and affections. And then usually, in spite of all I can do, my eyes will fill with tears because I have learned, all over again, what it really means to be back home.

*(My uncle survived my father by twenty years, but he too is gone now.)

2

The Fountain

Filled with Blood

All the Drakes were *big* Methodists; and Uncle John, Daddy's oldest brother, was a Methodist preacher. The Methodist Church in Woodville was a great big stone building that people said was Gothic. And it had big stained glass windows of Jesus and angels and the apostles; and I thought that if I finally did get to Heaven, I would want everything to look just like it did in those windows. The benches in the auditorium were real hard, though. They were originally supposed to have cushions in them; but before they got through building the church, they ran out of money. So for years everybody got stiff necks and strained backs from sitting in the old high-backed pews. Cousin Emma Moss declared they were responsible for her arthritis, but Daddy just said that was the best excuse for not going to church he had heard yet. Anyhow, the floors all had red carpets on them, and it was all pretty fine except for the pews. Fortunately, Mr. Peter B. Morris, an old bachelor who had a lot of money and was supposed to be an agnostic, didn't like the pews either. Mr. Morris came to church all the time with his sister; but, since he didn't like the pews and maybe because he was an agnostic, he sat out in the aisle in a chair that the ushers always left there for him. And finally, when he died, he left the church enough money to buy red velvet cushions for all the pews.

When I started to Sunday School, Miss Martha King was running the Beginners' Department. She lived down the street from us in a big white house that Mamma said had a Queen Anne front and a Mary Anne behind because it had been added on to so much, and I was crazy about her. Miss Martha told us stories out of the Bible, like about Abraham and Isaac, and Jacob's ladder, and Joseph's coat, and how Jesus made the blind man see. But the story I liked the best was about the shepherd who had lost one of his sheep and went out to look for it. The sheep's name was Rosemary, and the shepherd loved Rosemary so much that, even though all his other sheep were safe in the fold, he had to go out and try to find her. He looked a long time and was almost ready to go back home when he heard her crying way down in a ditch. She was hungry and scared, and he was awfully glad to find her; and he took his crook and pulled her out and took her up in his arms and carried her back to the fold. When she got to this part, Miss Martha would let the one that had learned the most memory verses take the big black walking cane that used to belong to Grandpa King and fish around in the waste basket, like he was the shepherd getting Rosemary out of the ditch. And I liked the songs we sang in Miss Martha's room, too. "Jesus Loves Me" was the first one I learned, and then "Praise Him, praise Him, all ye little children."

Then when I started to school, I was promoted to the Primary Department at Sunday School. And there we all sat in chairs that were just like the grown people's, only smaller; and we sang real *hymns* like "I Would Be True" and "Bringing in the Sheaves." My new Sunday School teacher was Miss Katherine Bond, and she was real young and pretty, with black hair and dark eyes and a very soft voice. She didn't have much trouble keeping us quiet, though, because we all thought she was so pretty that we didn't want to hurt her feelings for anything, and we really did try to behave.

After I got in the Primary Department, I started going to church with Mamma and Daddy. I liked the hymns, and I liked to sit where I could watch Annie Mae Lipscomb play the organ. Sometimes, I would put a hymnal on the rack behind the pew in front of me and make out like I was playing, too. And I would make all sorts of motions with my feet just like I was playing the organ pedals until Mamma looked at me to stop. I didn't usually listen to the sermon, though, because it didn't seem nearly so clear as the stories I heard in Sunday School; but all the grown people sat there looking mighty solemn, so I tried to look that way too.

But the part I liked best about church was the singing. I always liked "Come, Thou Fount of Every Blessing," even if I didn't know what it meant about raising your Ebenezer and melodious sonnets sung by flaming tongues above. But it sounded so grand and had a lot of zip to it, and Daddy said Grandma Drake used to always sing it to keep time by when she churned. But hymns were sort of funny. You were always calling yourself bad names like in "Amazing Grace," where you said you were a wretch, and "Alas, and did my Savior bleed," where you called yourself a worm. Or you were always singing about terrible things like in "There is a fountain filled with blood, drawn from Immanuel's veins." There was one verse of that hymn that I never did understand. It went:

The dying thief rejoiced to see
That fountain in his day;
And there may I, though vile as he,
Wash all my sins away.

But how could you wash anything away with blood, when blood wasn't really clean?

I didn't know what a lot of things in the sermon meant, either; but I didn't think it mattered right then because, after all, I was just a little boy. My nurse, Louella, had told me all about Heaven, where all the good people went when they died; and she said it was a pretty place where Jesus would lead me and take care of me always if I was good. Sometimes preachers talked about Hell, but Louella usually called it the Bad Place because *Hell* was supposed to be a bad word. It was hotter than any fire you could imagine, and anybody who had been bad enough to go there would burn forever and ever, and the Devil would stick his pitchfork in them just to make sure they were perfectly miserable. It sounded awful; but Louella said that if I was always good and minded Mamma and Daddy and didn't say ugly words or anything, I didn't need to worry about going there. Most of the time I didn't worry about it, but now and then I did when I got mad and talked ugly to Mamma and Daddy.

The part I really didn't like, either in sermons or hymns, though, was about Judgment Day. Every now and then Daddy sang an old song that ended: "O get ready, O get ready, for the Judgment Day." And every time he sang it, it made cold chills run up and down my spine because I was afraid that when Judgment Day came, I wouldn't go to Heaven. The saints and the sinners would be parted right and left, it said; and I was sure I would be in the bunch of sinners because it seemed like I never could get in the right group. When I was at school or even at a birthday party and there was any kind of game or race going on, I was nearly always the last one to come in; and I never could win a contest. I worried about it sometimes, but I was ashamed to tell Mamma and Daddy about it; I just hoped maybe Jesus would understand because He knew me so well, when it got my turn to go before the Great White Throne. I hated to think about it, though; and I didn't even like to hear them sing "When the roll is called up yonder" because it reminded me too much of that awful day when I would have to account for everything I had ever said or done.

Then one Sunday Miss Katherine asked us at Sunday School if we wouldn't like to go on and join the church. None of us had been baptized, and she said it was time for us to go on and be baptized and join the church. (I was supposed to have been baptized by Brother Cleanth Brooks, who had married Mamma and Daddy, but he had moved away to Louisiana before I was born.) I knew what happened when you were baptized, though. The preacher sprinkled some water on your head and said something about the Father, Son, and Holy Ghost that made you a full member of the church. Then you could go up to the Communion rail and take the Sacrament with everybody else on the first Sunday every month. Baptizing must be pretty important; but people were always making jokes about the Methodists sprinkling you and the Baptists ducking you under the water, only they called it immersion.

The Campbellites baptized by immersion, too, but they would die if you called them Campbellites. They were the Church of Christ, they said. People could make them perfectly furious by saying that their church had been started up by two men named Stone and Campbell. They would always swell up and say, "Our church was founded by Jesus Christ Himself. It's not like the Baptists, who say that John the Baptist established their church, or the Methodists, who haven't got anybody better than John Wesley that they can claim."

Well, anyhow, I went home and talked it all over with Mamma and Daddy; and they said, yes, it would be a good idea for me to go on and be baptized and join the church. They did want me to understand what I was getting into, though; so every afternoon after school I went to a class that Brother Morton, our preacher, was holding for all the boys and girls who were going to join the church. I told all the family what I was going to do, and they all said it was nice and they were proud of me, and Cousin Rosa Moss gave me a Bible of my very own.

It was springtime, and Brother Morton had decided that we would be taken into the church the Sunday afternoon after Easter. We had had lots of rain, and all the flowers were blooming. I never could remember when the world looked so beautiful before, and I thought it was very kind of God to make everything look so pretty just when I was getting ready to be baptized. One afternoon after I had come in from school, I decided to go down and see Mrs. Hargett, who lived down the street from us. She was a very kind woman who had a lot of children, all ages, and everybody used to like to go over to her house to play because the Hargetts always had so much fun. I always liked Polly, the youngest one, best because, even though she was several years older than I was, she didn't treat me like a baby. We were always playing dress-up and acting out movies we had seen. I knew the Hargetts were all Campbellites, but I thought Mrs. Hargett would be glad to hear about me being baptized anyway because all the Campbellites seemed to be great on baptizing folks. (Mamma had a cousin once that joined the Campbellite Church just to please her husband, who was one already. And when the time came for them to baptize her, she was sick in bed with the shingles; so the preacher just came to the house and baptized her in the tub.) So I went on down to Mrs. Hargett's, and Mamma was going to come down too after she had had her bath. All the shrubbery was in bloom, and you could smell the wisteria, that always made you feel sad and happy at the same time, everywhere. The sky was dark, but it wasn't going to rain; you could tell that by the way the clouds just hung there.

Mrs. Hargett was sitting on the porch in the swing darning some socks, so I just crawled up beside her and started talking. (All the children seemed to be gone.) We always talked about all sorts of things, and she never seemed to get tired of answering all the questions I asked her. I would ask her what made the weather or why different flowers smelled different from each other, and she would always say *something*. So we got to talking; and, all of a sudden, I said, "Mrs. Hargett, did you know that I am going to be baptized at the Methodist Church next Sunday afternoon?" And then I thought right away she would say how nice it was or something, like everybody else had said. But instead of that she didn't say anything for a minute; and then she said, "Well, you know, of course, that the Methodists don't really baptize anybody the right way."

I said, "What do you mean?" And she said, "Well, you know Christ was immersed; John the Baptist put Him all the way under the water. You can prove it by the Bible." I didn't like to dispute her word or anything; but I was beginning to feel sort of uneasy, so I said, "Well, isn't it just as good to do like the Methodists and sprinkle water on your head?" But she said, "Oh, no. Our church, the Church of Christ, is the only church that does it properly; so we don't believe that any baptism but ours does anybody any good."

There was a lump in my throat like I got when I was trying not to cry, only now I didn't feel like crying. I was afraid, but I didn't know exactly what of. But I had to go on. I said, "What do you mean by that?" Mrs. Hargett looked sort of funny, like she hated to say anything but she just had to. And she looked sort of satisfied, too, like she had something nobody else had. In a minute she spoke up and said, "Well, we just don't know what will happen to all the other denominations; but, as much as we hate to think it, they may not be saved."

My stomach sort of squinched up, and I thought I was really going to cry or be sick, but I didn't do either one. Suddenly, it seemed like something had happened to me that had been building up for a long time, something that, in a way, I ought to have known was going to happen. But I could hardly take it in: me, Robert Drake, in the Bad Place, just because I hadn't been baptized the right way. It didn't seem fair after all I had tried to mind Mamma and Daddy and get my lessons every day and everything. But if I was going to the Bad Place, Mamma and Daddy were too, and Miss Martha and Miss Katherine and everybody at the Methodist Church. I wanted to run home and grab Mamma around the neck and ask her what to do, but I didn't feel like that would help much because Mamma wasn't a Campbellite. But I wanted to go home anyhow. Suddenly, it seemed like a lot of things were beginning to make sense that I hadn't understood before—like about the foolish virgins that had the door shut in their faces and the rich man that Abraham wouldn't let Lazarus give any cold water to when he was down in the Bad Place. Was that going to happen to me, too?

Mrs. Hargett looked at me like she was waiting for something to happen, but I didn't really know what to say. After a while, I said, "Well, do you suppose it would be all right if I got them to baptize me at the Campbellite Church and then went on to the Methodist Church with Mamma and Daddy?" She looked sort of surprised and then smiled and said, "Well, I don't think that would do very much good because you wouldn't hear any of our sermons that way. And they are very important." That made me feel worse than ever. If it had been absolutely necessary, I thought I could have gone over to the Campbellite Church to be baptized, but I certainly didn't want to go to church regularly over there. They didn't have an organ or a piano or anything because, they said, it didn't say anything about them in the New Testament; so all their singing was done just dry-so, and sounded pretty much like it too.

Now I didn't know what to do. It was the first time in my life that I hadn't been able to ask Mamma what to do about something, but I knew it wasn't any use asking her because she was just a Methodist too. There seemed to be a big pit opening up down beneath me and coming on up into my stomach, and I felt like something terrible was going to happen to me. But I managed to hold on because Mrs. Hargett might say something even worse, and I felt I had to know what else was coming if it really was the truth, like she said. But she didn't say a word; she just kept on swinging and sewing.

Finally, I saw Mamma coming down the street, and I was so glad to see her that I ran down to the front steps and just hollered at her across the street: "Mamma, Mrs. Hargett says that only the Campbellites baptize people the right way, so I may not get to Heaven if I'm baptized at the Methodist Church. What in the world are we going to do?" I wanted her to tell me something right away and make it all right. But she didn't say anything. She just stood there with her fresh cotton dress and white shoes on, smiling across at Mrs. Hargett, and said, "Mrs. Hargett, Robert's going to be baptized Sunday at the church, and he's very excited about it. I hope he hasn't been bothering you." Mrs. Hargett was standing up now, looking across the street at Mamma like she might be waiting for something. Then I broke in and said, "But, Mamma, Mrs. Hargett said. . . . " But Mamma just said, "Come along, sonny-boy, I've got to get supper ready for your Daddy. Mrs. Hargett, come to see us." So I went on over and walked back up the street with her.

The days went by, and I hated to tell Mamma and Daddy that I was worried about joining the Methodist Church; they didn't seem to act like there was anything to worry about. There wasn't anybody else for me to ask about it that I could think of, so I just went on feeling worse and worse. The day before the service I was miserable. Maybe I was going to do something wrong and sinful, and I was worried and scared. But, then, what else could I do, after I'd told all the family and everybody? When I didn't eat my pie at dinner, Mamma asked me what the matter was. I thought I might as well go on and tell her, even if she was a Methodist. So I said, "Oh, Mamma, I'm afraid I'm not going to be baptized the right way, and I'll go to the Bad Place when I die." Mamma said, "Now, Robert, you know that's a lot of foolishness. All our family are Methodists, and your Uncle John is a Methodist preacher. Don't you know that Daddy and I wouldn't let you do anything wrong?" And I said, "Yes, Mamma, but Mrs. Hargett said. . . . " But Mamma broke in right quick and said, "Now, you don't have to listen to anybody but Mamma and Daddy, and we say it's all right for you to go on and join the Methodist Church."

But suppose Mamma and Daddy were wrong. Such an idea had never entered my mind before, and now I didn't know what to say. I just sat at the table and played with my food. After a while Mamma got up and said, "Come out on the front porch with me for a minute," so I got up and followed her. She stood there and pointed over towards Cousin Rosa and Cousin Emma's house and said, "Suppose you wanted to go from here over to see Cousin Rosa and Cousin Emma. You could go around by Dr. Wilson's house up on the corner, or you could go round the other way by the grammar school. But you would get there just the same. Now, churches are just like that. All of us are trying to get to the same place, whether we get there or not. Some churches try to go one way and some, another. But we are all working for the same goal. Do you see what I mean?" I said yes, even though I wasn't sure this had cleared up everything that had been bothering me. But I didn't want Mamma to know that I doubted her word about anything. I just guessed God would understand the trouble I was in and maybe make some allowance for it.

So late Sunday afternoon I was baptized at the Communion rail in the Methodist Church, with Mamma and Daddy and Miss Katherine Bond standing behind me. It was a dark, wet day; it was cold, too, the kind of day that makes people say, "You know, you can freeze to death in the spring of the year." As soon as Brother Morton had baptized me, I felt wonderfully clean and like I was sort of starting all over again. I wanted to tell everybody about how good I felt, but I knew I couldn't right there in church. But after the service we went down to see Mr. Jim Loyd, who had been real sick but was getting better; and I was glad because I wanted to tell *somebody* how I felt. I had almost forgotten about Mrs. Hargett and the Campbellites.

Somebody had sent Mr. Loyd some sweet peas; they were very fresh and pretty, with drops of rainwater still on them. I thought, "I am just like those sweet peas. Now that my sins have been washed away, I don't have to worry about anything any more. I have been baptized in water, just like those sweet peas." But then, all of a sudden, I remembered about the fountain filled with blood, and I wondered whether you would get to Heaven quicker if you were baptized in blood, and not just *sprinkled* with it but *immersed* in it—plunged beneath that flood, like it said in the hymn; and maybe *water* was no good anyhow. All these things seemed to be a lot different from the sweet peas, but they seemed more real in a way.

Suddenly, I broke into the grown folks' conversation and said, "Did you all know I was baptized at the Methodist Church this afternoon?" I just had to say it to keep from thinking about Mrs. Hargett and the blood and the Bad Place, which all seemed to be mixed up together in my mind. And then everybody spoke up and said, "Isn't that nice?" or "How sweet!" like I knew they would. But it didn't seem to matter any more. I wanted to run outside into the rain, to get somewhere where I could forget about Mrs. Hargett and everything else, but I knew it wouldn't do any good.

I went over to the window and looked out at the rain coming down on Miss Jessie Loyd's spring flowers. I had always liked the rain because it made the flowers grow and it felt so good on your skin in the springtime, like it was washing everything clean all over. Inside the room everything was real snug and warm, and everybody was talking, and there was a lot of smoke from the big cigar Daddy was smoking. But outside the sky was dark, and the rain seemed like it wasn't ever going to stop.

3

Good Morning,

Merry Sunshine

When I started to school, Cousin Rosa Moss was my teacher. She had taught the first grade for nearly forty years, and everyone in Woodville had started to school to her. In fact, one time the Rotarians all got together and gave Cousin Rosa a wrist watch and said they were going to rename the Primary School, where she taught, the Rosa Moss School. But most people still called it the Little School, not because it was little itself but because it was where the little folks started to school.

I thought I better not call her Cousin Rosa when I was in school; it didn't seem exactly fair to the other children. So I just called her Miss Rosa like everybody else. The other first-grade teacher was Miss Beersheba Hall (she was named after somebody in the Bible), and she was terribly strict and made you keep as quiet as mice. She had a piano in her room, but Cousin Rosa had a real reed organ. And every now and then when we were tired and restless from sitting so long, she would go back to the organ and play for us to march around the room, usually the "Black Hawk Waltz" or something like that. Sometimes we sang, and the song we learned that I liked best was "Good Morning, Merry Sunshine." It started off like this:

Good morning, merry sunshine!
Why did you wake so soon?
You scared away the little stars,
And shined away the moon.

Mamma had learned that song when she was a little girl, and sometimes she waked me up in the morning by calling out "Good morning, merry sunshine!" But the main reason I liked it was that it acted like the sun and the moon and the stars weren't so far away and terrible like some people were always telling you but they were sort of like you and you could feel friendly toward them and make out like you really were talking to them.

I didn't see how in the world I was ever going to learn to read; it didn't look like you could *ever* learn all that many separate words. But it seemed to come on sort of gradual and didn't hurt so much that way. Cousin Rosa started us out by learning all the letters and how they sounded: "T" was how a streetcar sounded when it stopped and went "tick-tick-tick." And then we started learning whole words, which Cousin Rosa would hold up on great big cards.

And then finally we were ready to start on the preprimer. We were really going to start reading. Cousin Rosa divided us into two classes because she couldn't handle but so many at the time around the big reading table up in front of the room. And every day when it came time for reading, we would go up and read out of the pre-primers that said on the front *Elson-Gray Basic Readers*. They were all about a family with three children named Dick, Jane, and Baby. On the first page was a picture of Dick running; and underneath it said, "Dick. See Dick run." On the next page there was a picture of Jane running; and down under the picture it said, "Jane. See Jane run. Run, Jane, run." That's the way it would always do; every time it looked like it would tell you one more thing. But Mamma said that was the way school was; every day you had to learn something new so you could learn something new the next day. It looked to me like you would get right tired of *always* having to learn something new every day as long as you were in school. And, then, after you got out of school, it looked like you had to work till you died. But Mamma said that was the way it had to be.

When we went up to read, Cousin Rosa sat in a big half-moon that was cut into the table so she could be closer to all of us and maybe even reach across and use her ruler on us when we misbehaved. One day she even gave Tommy Whitley a paddling because he told her he had lost his reader and she found out he had torn it up so he wouldn't have to read any more. That scared me nearly to death because it was the first time she had ever whipped anybody, and I was afraid she might start to making it a general rule. So I decided maybe I better go home.

So I asked Cousin Rosa if I could be excused, and she said yes. But I didn't do a thing but go down in the basement and get my coat and start for home. Our house was two blocks from the school, and I had gotten about halfway home when I began to think about what Mamma would say about me leaving right in the middle of class. Mamma believed the worst thing in the world was not doing what you were supposed to do—no matter what. She was always talking about *fulfilling your obligations,* and it seemed like that meant anything from going to Sunday School every Sunday to having the Wednesday Bridge Club when it was your time. I felt like Mamma would say I wasn't fulfilling my obligations; and you had to do that no matter if it killed you because, if people didn't fulfill their obligations, there just wouldn't be any world. (That's what Mamma said.) So I decided I'd better go on back, and I was able to slip back into the classroom without Cousin Rosa knowing I had been anywhere but to the rest room.

The rest rooms were down in the basement, where we played and ate our lunches when it was bad outside. Also, when it was bad, we would line up downstairs to come back up after recess. Mrs. Martin, one of the second-grade teachers, would come down and ring a big dinner bell, and everybody would form a line. Then Miss Beersheba would play "The Stars and Stripes Forever" on the piano in her room, and we would all march upstairs. Sometimes Cousin Rosa or Miss Annie Kate Barnes, the other second-grade teacher, would play the march; but usually it was just Miss Beersheba. After all, it was *her* piano.

When we ate lunch down in the basement, you got to see what everybody else was eating. And I was real glad because nobody else had pineapple sandwiches like I did. Mamma would take a big cookie cutter and cut out the bread in a circle just as big as a slice of pineapple, and I thought that kind of pineapple sandwich tasted a lot better than when it was just stuck between two regular slices of bread. Every morning Cousin Rosa would ask how many of us wanted white milk and how many wanted chocolate, and we all held up our hands for the different things. And just before dinner time the colored boy from Jackson's Dairy would bring in exactly as many bottles as we needed. I thought it was wonderful that it always came out even like that.

The basement was where Uncle Urshel stayed most of the time. His name was Uncle Urshel Vance, and he was the colored janitor. His wife was Aunt Susanna, and she had been Mamma's washwoman since before she and Daddy married. Uncle Urshel and Aunt Susanna had a daughter named Lady Jane that taught in the colored grammar school and a son named Booker T. that lived over in North Carolina. Every summer when he came to see Uncle Urshel and Aunt Susanna, I would go down and play with Alice Ann, Booker T.'s little girl. Uncle Urshel and Aunt Susanna lived right on the railroad cut, and Alice Ann and I would sit out on the back porch eating ripe tomatoes that Aunt Susanna kept in the icebox until they were real cold and watch the trains go by.

Everybody knew Uncle Urshel was getting old, but nobody liked to say anything about it because he was so faithful and good and always had the furnace going so it would be good and warm when we got to school. And when somebody wet their pants, he would take you in and let you dry by the furnace without saying a word to anybody. But one day Beulah Mae Edwards from out at Four Points that always smelled bad got mad at Uncle Urshel because he wouldn't let her chunk coal from the coal pile at Darlene Varner and called him a nasty old black nigger. Cousin Rosa happened to be coming down the steps at the time; and she didn't do a thing but take Beulah Mae by the hand and lead her to the rest room and wash her mouth out with soap, which was probably what Mamma would have done to me if she had ever caught me saying a thing like that. (Uncle Urshel died not long after I went on over to the big grammar school, and I heard Cousin Rosa tell Mamma that Aunt Susanna didn't keep him out but three days—most of the Negroes kept their dead folks out at least a week—and that just proved what superior Negroes the Vances were.)

Part of learning to read, of course, was learning to spell, and we used to line up every day for spelling class and have headmarks and trapping, too. I always had more headmarks than anybody else; but I didn't think that was unusual because if you fulfilled your obligations and learned your spelling lesson *perfectly* every day, it was bound to be that way. So along toward the end of the year when Cousin Rosa announced that we were going to have a spelling match with Miss Beersheba's room, I didn't think much about it; I felt like I would probably win.

Well, the day for the spelling match finally came around, and we all went into Miss Beersheba's room and lined up on the side of the room with the piano. Her children were already lined up along the other side, and so we started off. People began to miss words and have to sit down, and the words kept getting harder so more people had to sit down. Finally, there wasn't anybody but me left on Cousin Rosa's side, and nobody but John Edgar Botts on Miss Beersheba's. John Edgar was from out at Haley's Switch, and he brought his lunch to school every day in a paper sack and his milk in a little jar. When you were choosing up sides for anything, John Edgar was nearly always the last one to be chosen, but he kept right on wanting to play. He never did say much, but that didn't keep him from listening every time you were talking about what you had seen at the picture show on Saturday or whether or not you were going to get to go to Ringling Brothers Circus when it came to Memphis. I didn't see why John Edgar didn't quit listening around; it didn't seem to me like he had anything to listen *about* if he never went anywhere or did anything.

Well, anyhow, there John Edgar and I were standing up there looking each other in the face, and Miss Beersheba kept giving out harder and harder words. I would always spell mine right off because the more you thought about it, the more mixed up you got. But John Edgar would always wait until you thought sure he didn't know how to spell the word, and then he would spell it out real slow like he knew exactly what he was doing and was enjoying taking his time about it.

Finally, Miss Beersheba looked at me and said "about." I wasn't sure exactly how it went, but I didn't want to get all up in the air trying to decide, so I just spoke up and said "a-b-o-u-g-h-t." But Miss Beersheba said, "No, that's wrong. John Edgar, can you spell it?" And John Edgar sort of smiled real slow like he wanted to drag it out as long as he could; then he spelled "a-b-o-u-t." And Miss Beersheba said, "That's right. John Edgar wins!"

And then everybody clapped for John Edgar, and John Edgar clapped for himself, too. I wanted to go over and hit him; but I wanted to cry, too, so the only thing I could do was clap like everybody else. It didn't seem right for John Edgar to win after I had worked so hard fulfilling my obligations. What would Mamma say?

And then he had to clap for himself on top of all that; he didn't know any better, I reckoned.

I was perfectly miserable, standing there wondering what had gone wrong to keep me from winning and wondering what Cousin Rosa would tell Mamma and what everybody would say. But then Miss Beersheba said while we were all in her room, we would all sing some songs; and she went over and sat down at the piano. Just before we started to sing, though, Cousin Rosa came up and put her arm around me and whispered, "I'm just as proud of you as I can be because you did your best." But I didn't understand that. Why didn't you win if you did your best? Why didn't you win if you fulfilled your obligations? But then I thought maybe John Edgar had fulfilled his obligations, too, and I didn't know what to make of it.

Then Miss Beersheba started in on "Good Morning, Merry Sunshine," and I began to think about the words.

> Good morning, merry sunshine!
> Why did you wake so soon?
> You scared away the little stars,
> And shined away the moon.

Maybe it was sort of like the sun and moon and stars that had different times to do things, the sun in the daytime and the moon and stars at night. Maybe they were all fulfilling their obligations, but maybe their obligations were all different. Maybe people had to work that way, too. I thought about it a minute, and then I began to sing as loud as anybody else.

4

Easy Steps

for Little Feet

One day when I was about five years old, Mamma came in from up at Cousin Rosa Moss' and said she had brought me a new story book. And I was glad because we had about run out of Grimm's fairy tales. This wasn't really a *new* book; it was just new to me. Because it used to belong to Mamma when she was a little girl, and Cousin Rosa had been just borrowing it to read out of to her first-grade children.

It was a big, thick, gray book with the title done in gold letters with lots of curlicues on the front. It was called *Easy Steps for Little Feet*, and what it was, was Bible stories. Inside there were a lot of dark-looking pictures to show what was going on in the stories, that Mamma said were steel engravings. And I thought that was a good name for them because they did look sort of cold and steely and like they didn't care whether you looked at them or not because, after all, they *were* in the Bible, and proud *of* it.

Whoever made the pictures seemed to be real fond of showing angels coming down to straighten people out and make them mind, like the one that was leading Adam and Eve out of the Garden of Eden. He was sort of sailing over them in the air, pointing on ahead to where they were going with one hand and reaching down and leading Adam with the other. (Adam had Eve by his other hand, but the angel wasn't having anything to do with *her*.) You couldn't tell whether the angel was a man or a woman, but somehow he always seemed like a man even if he did have long hair. You could tell how he felt about it all by the way he looked. He wasn't exactly *enjoying* himself, but he *was* doing his duty like grown people were always talking about. And they were real great on that, especially when the *duty* part was all on your side. So the angel didn't look proud or glad or anything like that; he just looked like he was gwine where he was gwine, as my nurse Louella used to say.

There was another picture that I used to look at a lot. It was where Abraham was fixing to sacrifice Isaac just because God had told him to, just to try him out. I never had thought God was playing fair about that anyhow, trying to find out how much Abraham loved him by making him choose between his little boy and Himself. But what made me mad was the way Abraham looked. He was holding Isaac's hands together with his left hand so Isaac couldn't fight back, and he was holding the knife up in the air in his right hand and looking up in the sky like he was trying to show God that he was doing exactly what He wanted. And I thought Abraham looked like he was gwine where he was gwine, too; and it was all right for him because he was minding God, but it was kind of hard on Isaac.

Mamma started reading me a Bible story nearly every day, and I began to feel like Miss Eunice Grace Patterson, who was the lady that wrote *Easy Steps for Little Feet,* was talking about a different bunch of people than Miss Martha King, who was my Sunday School teacher. Miss Martha was always telling us about how Jesus had been a little child just like we were. And He would help his father, Joseph, in the carpenter shop because He was supposed to do what His mother and father said, too. And then she would tell about how He still loved little children when He got to be a grown man and had lots of other things to worry about. Even then He said, "Suffer little children to come unto Me."

The stories were all pretty much along the same line; they were all about what happened to people that misbehaved, like Adam and Eve, or Lot's wife, or Nebuchadnezzar, or somebody like that. Of course, you knew the people that minded God were going to come out on top, but you couldn't help feeling sorry for the people that were trying to have a good time while they could because you knew that wasn't a drop in the bucket to the bad time they were going to have in Eternity. And sometimes the people on God's side seemed like such show-offs, like Shadrach, Meshach, and Abednego parading around in the fiery furnace or Joshua blowing the trumpet at Jericho.

Miss Eunice Grace Patterson never did have much to say about King David that Miss Martha used to tell us about killing Goliath and all. I liked him right well because he didn't seem as prissy as a lot of the good people did, but Miss Eunice Grace Patterson usually just referred to him as the Psalmist, and that didn't seem right when you knew he had certainly been doing something all those years besides writing a hundred and fifty psalms. She did say one time that King David was a good example of how the people God loved best could stray from the fold; but when I asked Mamma about it, she just said, well, he didn't always act as pretty when he got grown up as he did when he was out taking care of those sheep.

The story that used to worry me the most, though, was about Noah and the ark. Miss Eunice Grace Patterson told all about how God came down and told Noah that He was going to destroy the world with a great flood because everybody was acting so ugly, but He was going to save Noah and his family because Noah was so good. So Noah had to go to work and build an ark large enough for them and every kind of animal on earth to be saved in. And there was a picture of Noah and his sons building away at the ark while all their neighbors sat around making fun of them for doing something so silly. And Noah looked like he was gwine where he was gwine, too.

And then Miss Eunice Grace Patterson told about how it rained for forty days and nights and everybody but Noah and his family and all their animals was drowned. And I could tell she didn't much care about Noah's neighbors that had laughed at him so, but I did because I felt like most people would be on her side anyhow and *somebody* had to feel sorry for them, even if they were bad.

Then she went on to tell about how after God had got everybody drowned real good, He stopped the rain, and the water finally went down and the ark came to rest on dry land. And Noah and his family all got out and gave thanks that they had been spared, even though they had known all along they were going to be. And then God put a rainbow up in the sky to show everybody that He wasn't ever going to do *that* any more; the next time He was going to use *fire*. I didn't see that it made much difference one way or the other; God was going to get you in the end. I used to worry about it a lot because it looked like I didn't ever really *want* to be good anyhow, and I didn't reckon I could ever really keep the Ten Commandments. And Miss Eunice Grace Patterson had certainly shown what happened to you when you didn't. (Somehow I thought she and Moses would have gotten along fine.)

I never did say anything to Mamma about the way Miss Eunice Grace Patterson worried me. After all, she couldn't tell me it was just a story like when I cried because Bluebeard was going to cut his wife's head off; this was the Bible. But Mamma must have guessed how I felt because when we finished *Easy Steps for Little Feet* (it ended with the two she-bears eating up the little children that had made fun of Elisha), she started in on *Alice in Wonderland*.

In a few years I was able to read the Bible for myself. And I found out that there were a good many stories that Miss Eunice Grace Patterson had left out, especially in the New Testament. And I finally got so I could look at steel engravings without going all cold in the bottom of my stomach. But I still never did really care much about rainbows.

5

The First Funeral

I never had been to a funeral before, but I had heard all about them. Miss Sara Palmer, who lived across the street from us, had died the year before, and I could watch all the things going on over there—the flowers going in from Miss Sophie Caldwell's flower shop and Waterfield and Hill's hearse driving up to take Miss Sara to the cemetery. Miss Sara's little girl, Anne, was my age; and I was sorry that her mother was dead. When I asked Mamma why she died, she said, "Well, she just couldn't get well."

I knew that when people died, they put them in a casket made out of metal or wood and dug a grave and buried them. But first they had to have a funeral. Sometimes after a big funeral Mamma and Daddy and I would drive by the cemetery to look at the flowers. But now I was really going to a funeral. Daddy's old friend, Mr. Henry Seaton, had died out at Maple Grove, and they were going to have the funeral at Wesley Church and bury him in the churchyard there. That was several miles away from Maple Grove, but we were going by Mr. Seaton's house beforehand.

Maple Grove was the community about three miles out of Woodville where all of Mamma and Daddy's people had first settled when they came to Tennessee. We went back there every Sunday afternoon to see Pa Drake, my grandfather, who was a Confederate veteran but was real old and feeble now and lived with Uncle Jim and Aunt Mary. Sometimes we would go to Maple Grove Church to preaching. Uncle Jim and Aunt Mary's daughter, Lina, played the piano for church, and I liked to hear everybody sing all the hymns like "Will there be any stars in my crown?" and "He included me" that we never seemed to sing in Woodville. The church burned acetylene lamps, though everybody else out there didn't have anything but coal oil lamps for light. The acetylene lamps sputtered a lot and made a sort of spooky light, but that seemed to me the right kind of light to have in church. In the very back of the church was a long steel rod, running across from one corner on the floor to the opposite corner on the ceiling. It was supposed to keep the church from being blown away by the wind. A lot of people out at Maple Grove even had storm houses because years ago there had been a big storm out there that blew away a lot of houses and trees.

But Mr. Seaton's funeral was going to be at Wesley Church, and I was glad we were going because I never had been there before. It was a very hot day in July and it was Thursday, the day all the stores in town were closed in the summer. There hadn't been any rain in a long time, and we stirred up a big cloud of dust as we drove through the country on the gravel road. Long before we reached Mr. Seaton's house we could see a lot more dust, rising where all the cars had turned off the road into his driveway.

Mamma said that the body was still at the house. I wanted to know what that was; and she said, "Mr. Seaton, Robert." I said, "Well, why don't you call him that?" And she said, "Because he's dead." I didn't see any reason to call him something else, especially something that sounded like a *thing*, just because he was dead. Mr. Seaton's wife was dead, and he lived by himself with only some of his kinfolks to come see about him now and then. They said he had died of pneumonia, and I thought that was funny because it was summertime and pneumonia was what you were always afraid of catching in the winter.

When we finally drove up in front of the house, we parked along in a row with all the other cars. There were pots of ferns on the front porch, and I noticed that they needed watering. I thought maybe they needed some tea water poured on them, like Cousin Emma Moss always used on her ferns; but I didn't say anything about it. The house was low on the ground and didn't have any underpinning, so you could see the chickens running in and out to get under there where it was cool. They made soft purring noises, and now and then one of the hens would let out a squawk. But for the most part things were quiet, and I wondered why you couldn't hear any talking going on in the house. You could hear people moving around in there the way you can in a house without any underpinning—short, quick steps that stopped all of a sudden like something very important was just over and done with and they had gotten there too late. The house had a tin roof, and the sun was blazing down on it like fire.

We could hardly get in the screen door, there were so many people there. I never did see the casket. I was thinking that maybe I might run into Mr. Seaton before I knew it, and I wasn't sure I wanted to. From inside the window I could hear a cheeping noise, and I noticed a cage of canaries, little canaries that had just been hatched and didn't seem to know or care that there was about to be a funeral going on. Then I looked over in a corner and saw Cousin Bernice White smiling at me. She was a cousin of Mamma's, and Mamma always said that she was the scariest mortal that had ever breathed, and I wondered why if she was so scary she had come to a funeral. My colored nurse, Louella, was afraid of dead folks, but it didn't seem to me like they would hurt you. I wanted to ask Cousin Bernice why she had come to the funeral, but I thought maybe that would sound impolite. So I just went over and stood in front of her and smiled, hoping she would tell me. She said, "We certainly do miss Lina out here now. With her studying the piano in Chicago this summer, the church doesn't seem the same." I said, "Oh, but she'll be back in a month, won't she?" And Cousin Bernice said she reckoned she would.

Mamma and Daddy were acting in a way I had never seen them before. They were walking around on tiptoe talking very quietly to people. I didn't exactly understand it, but I thought it must have something to do with death. But if Mr. Seaton had really gone to Heaven, talking wasn't going to bother him one way or the other. I got awfully restless because there didn't seem to be anybody much for me to talk to. I wanted to ask Aunt Mary when Lina was coming home, but I couldn't find her anywhere.

Finally, people began to clear their throats and scrape their split-bottom chairs back against the wall. I thought it must be time to go, and I was glad. The smell of all those hothouse flowers and the hot sun beating down on that tin roof didn't make me feel very good. Then I looked outside the window, and there was Waterfield and Hill's hearse pulled right up in front of the front door. Waterfield and Hill ran a combination furniture store and undertaking business. The furniture was downstairs, and the undertaking went on upstairs. They put on all the funerals in Woodville, and they had a big square-looking black hearse that all the Negroes called "Mr. Waterfield-Hill's hearse."

The six men who were carrying the casket out to the hearse were called pallbearers, but I wasn't sure exactly why. Mamma said that the family's big blanket of flowers on top of the casket was called the pall; but it looked like it was more Mr. Seaton they were carrying than the pall. Daddy wasn't a pallbearer, so we just went out and got in the car to be ready when the procession started. I wasn't sure exactly what I ought to be doing now. I knew that people cried at funerals because after all if you put somebody away in the ground, you never would see them again. But nobody seemed to be crying today. Maybe that was because Mr. Seaton didn't leave a wife and a lot of children behind. I sort of felt like maybe I should cry, but I decided that maybe I didn't have any real reason since I didn't even know what Mr. Seaton looked like.

We started off in the procession very slow. It was almost like a Christmas pageant when the shepherds and Wise Men moved real solemnly across the stage to the manger because they were afraid of tripping over their costumes. But it wasn't Christmas now; it was hot as fire. Mamma and Daddy and I were riding in the front seat of the car, and it seemed like we were sort of sealed up inside with all the hot air. It wasn't more than six miles to Wesley Church, but it took us more than half an hour to get there.

I was awfully glad to see the church, finally, rising up in a grove of oak and cedar trees. It was a white weatherboarded building, and it was perfectly plain except for the pointed windows that churches always seemed to have. They didn't have colored pictures on them of Jesus and the angels like ours did at home, though. They were just plain milk-white, like bathroom windows.

When we finally got inside the church, the men from Waterfield and Hill's rolled the casket up the aisle and placed it at the foot of the pulpit. Then they opened it and put a veil over it, sort of like a bride's veil, I thought. I was very much interested in weddings and went to all the ones Mamma would take me to. And all the children in our neighborhood used to get together and put on weddings on our front porch. We played on the little toy piano Santa Claus had brought me, and we used an old lace curtain of

Mamma's for the veil. Sometimes we used some of her white althaeas for the bouquet, if she wasn't going to use them herself.

But now there weren't any althaeas (Mamma usually called
them rose of Sharon); there were only hothouse flowers like gla-
dioli, carnations, and lilies. Even with all the windows open, the
church was very hot, and the odor of all the flowers almost made
me sick at my stomach. Finally the quartet and the pianist came in
and got up on the rostrum. Then the Woodville circuit preacher
came in and stood up there in the pulpit right where he could look
down into Mr. Seaton's face if he wanted to. Somehow I thought
if it was me, I'd just as soon not have that casket open. The quartet
sang "Safe in the Arms of Jesus"; then the preacher prayed a long
prayer, thanking God for the good life Mr. Seaton had lived and
saying how glad they all were that he was now in Heaven with
Jesus and all his own folks. Some of the women began to cry; a lot
of babies began to cry, too, not knowing what was the matter.

Then the quartet sang "In the Sweet By and By," and the
preacher began his talk—all about what a good man Mr. Seaton had
been and how they would all miss him. Now the crying was louder,
and I thought how strange it was that all those people were crying
about Mr. Seaton and they weren't even any kin to him. I looked
at Mamma and Daddy, but they were looking straight ahead. Neither one of them showed any signs of wanting to cry, but then they
always kept very straight faces on important occasions. Maybe
some people just didn't ever cry, no matter how bad they felt. But
this was certainly the saddest occasion I had ever been to, and I
thought maybe I ought to be crying. About that time I looked
around and there was Cousin Bernice looking at me, and she
seemed to know how I felt because she smiled at me. I thought she
couldn't be so very scary if she knew how I felt. But I didn't say
anything and tried to think about all the flowers up on the rostrum
until the service was over.

At the end of his talk the preacher announced that while the
quartet sang the last hymn, those who wished could come up and
view the remains. The people started filing by the casket to look at
Mr. Seaton for the last time. Some of them even stopped and cried
over him, but their families pulled them on along. I looked at
Mamma and Daddy to see what they were going to do, but they
sat perfectly still. I later heard Mamma say she thought it was per-

fectly heathen to do such a thing, but right then I thought maybe she might go up to see Mr. Seaton. Mamma always liked to know what was going on and keep up with things. But she and Daddy didn't go, and I was sort of glad because I thought I had just as soon not look at Mr. Seaton, even though he did have a bride's veil over him.

Then finally when everybody had been up that was going to, the men from Waterfield and Hill's stepped up real quiet and closed down the casket; then we all got ready to go into the churchyard for the burial. (They always called it the "interment" on the black-bordered funeral notices that were distributed in the stores around the Square when anybody in Woodville died.) It was real cool out under the cedar trees but pretty dark and gloomy. I noticed that a lot of tombstones were streaked with a stain where the rain water had run off the cedars onto them. I had heard Mamma say once that Colonel Harris, who gave the land for the cemetery at home, specified in the deed that no cedar trees should ever be planted there. I guess he thought they looked too gloomy, but the stain may have had something to do with it, too.

Everybody stood around close to the grave, and the undertaker's men put a blanket of artificial grass and the pall on top of the casket, and it sank into the grave almost like magic. The preacher started the burial service, but I didn't pay much attention to him. I was looking around at all the names on the tombstones and wondering how long it would be before my name was on a tombstone and if Mr. Seaton would like it down there even if he wasn't supposed to know anything about it. How would he feel even in Heaven when his body started to turn to dust again?

Then, while the preacher pronounced the benediction, I looked off across the cemetery and saw the undertaker's men standing apart from the crowd under a big cedar tree. It was right at noon, so they weren't getting much shade. I whispered to Mamma and asked her what they were doing there and why they weren't with the rest of the crowd. And she said, "They are waiting for everybody to go away so they can complete the burying."

I said, "But they have already buried him. See, the casket is down in the ground." But she said, "This is only a sort of imitation burial. After we leave, they will take the artificial grass and the flowers off the casket and put dirt on top of it permanently."

I said, "Well, why don't they do it now? Why are they trying to hide the real burial?" And she said, "Well, some people think it's nicer this way. You don't have to hear the sound of the dirt falling on the casket. That's a sound that makes some people feel mighty sad." It looked to me like they were trying to fool Mr. Seaton and everybody else into thinking they really weren't putting him in the ground. I didn't like it because it didn't seem fair, in a way. It was sort of like calling Mr. Seaton "the body" or saying "pass away" for "die."

After the service we stopped to speak to a lot of people that Mamma and Daddy knew from around in the county. Of course, we ran into Cousin Hattie Burks, who went to every funeral in that part of the world, Mamma said. She was Mamma's cousin, and every time she saw me, she would say, "I'll bet you don't know who I am." And I would have to say, "Yes, I do, you're Cousin Hattie Burks." And then she would say, "That's right, and you are Lucille's child." Daddy had been kin to her husband, Cousin Hiram Burks; and he said Cousin Hattie was one of the best women he ever saw but she could talk the legs off a brass mule. Now Cousin Hattie said, "I declare, when you think of Henry Seaton going this way, it makes you realize we're all getting on. Pretty soon there won't be many of us old hands left." I could tell Mamma didn't exactly like what Cousin Hattie said, but she just sort of smiled and shook her head and asked Cousin Hattie when she was coming to see us.

After a while we got back in the car to go home. The sun was high overhead, but you could hardly see anything to the right or left because the woods were so dense. It was awfully hot, and Mamma's voile dress was sticking to her in places. I was thinking about the field peas cooked with side meat we were going to have for dinner. I asked Mamma how many helpings I could have, but she seemed only to halfway hear me, like she was thinking about something else. Daddy didn't say much either. He just looked at the road like he never had driven on it before and had to be mighty careful. I didn't believe they were thinking about the funeral; they hadn't seemed to be very upset about it.

After a while we came out of the woods into the cotton fields, and then the sun was shining down right on us out of a blazing blue sky. I kept on asking questions about dinner and what we were going to do after that until finally Mamma said, "Goodness, Robert, don't you ever run down? Daddy, see if you can turn him off." But Daddy said, "Oh, leave him alone, Mamma. He's only a little boy." And then we rode along with nobody saying anything for a couple of miles; and I began to wonder if they had now finally gotten Mr. Seaton into the ground for good, with all that dirt on top of him.

6

The Moss Girls

Cousin Rosa and Cousin Emma Moss were Mamma's two old-maid cousins who lived up on the corner by the railroad bridge. When we sat out on their porch in the summertime, you could hardly talk, the trains made so much noise chugging through the cut. Mamma didn't like having to talk between trains; but they were used to it and would always laugh and say, "There are always more trains when Lucille comes." In the daytime there was a big morning-glory vine that helped keep off the sun. Sometimes it was plain blue, but then sometimes it was the Scarlett O'-Hara kind that had big red blooms.

Cousin Emma grew all the flowers and did the housework because Cousin Rosa taught school. She had taught the first grade for nearly fifty years, and she said she never had needed second sight because she hadn't lost the first yet. Mr. Sam Chism, who was superintendent of the Baptist Sunday School, said that was because she never had read anything but the first reader, and that had real large print. When anybody reminded her of that, she would die laughing and say, "Sam Chism ought to be shot."

At night when we sat out on the front porch up there and everybody was talking so low that you could hear the July flies screeching and all the quiet noises coming from the Negro houses around the corner, you always had time to notice things more; and one thing would be the citronella that Cousin Rosa used to keep off the mosquitoes. But Cousin Emma didn't like it. She would say, "Rosa acts such a fool about that smelly old stuff. I don't think it does anything but draw more mosquitoes. How can you expect anything to improve this porch when we get that filthy old train smoke all day long? If I could dispose of Sister, I'd sell this house in a minute."

But we all knew she wouldn't live anywhere else for the world. She and Cousin Rosa had lived there ever since Uncle Forrest and Aunt Bessie had moved to town years ago from out in the country. Mamma said Aunt Bessie used to say, "Lucille, I don't know what will become of the girls when I die. They're spoiled rotten." And Mamma said the Lord knew that was true enough, but they got along all right somehow. Sometimes they had roomers living with them, but every now and then they would decide they didn't want any more of them and would have all the house to themselves. But Auntee said it was just because they each wanted a room to pout in.

Auntee, who was really Cousin Kate Parker, was their first cousin, and she lived with them. Her mother had died when she was two years old; and she had always lived part the time with Cousin Rosa and Cousin Emma until she married Mr. Parker, who was old enough to be her father. After he died, she came back to live with them; and they still treated her like she was two years old. They still called her "Kate Moss" like she hadn't ever been married. But she had all right; you could see two of Mr. Parker's big diamond rings right there on her hands. I used to ask her why she didn't have the stones reset in a lady's ring; and she would say, "Aw, honey, look at Auntee's big old hands. A little old ring like that wouldn't look right on me." But I think she didn't want to change them because Mr. Parker had worn them, even if he was old enough to be her father.

All the neighbors called the three of them "the Moss girls," and you could see them riding all over the county most any time in Cousin Rosa's little blue Ford. She had tried to drive it herself over the protests of all the family, but finally she just gave up and let Auntee take the wheel. But that wasn't until after she had climbed the bank and almost come up on the porch where Cousin Emma was reading a continued story in the *Ladies' Home Journal*. Cousin Emma wasn't interested in driving, but she was a powerful big rider. Auntee said she wanted to go every time the wheel turned. It didn't matter where you were going; Cousin Emma just liked to *go.*

Cousin Rosa was a tall, loose-jointed woman; you never would have thought of her as being young and pretty. But she had been handsome when she was younger, Mamma said. Now she had had asthma and pernicious anemia so long that she looked sort of yellow, and her skin was all wrinkled, too. Auntee used to call her "Limber" because she was so awkward, but Cousin Emma said that was because the anemia had affected her circulation and she didn't have any feeling in her feet. Mamma said she just knew Cousin Rosa was going to fall and break her hip one day, and then what in the world would they do with her? But Cousin Emma said that wouldn't be nearly as bad as the day she got false teeth.

Cousin Emma was a lot smaller than Cousin Rosa, and I used to think she was older because her hair was so much grayer. She was really several years younger than Cousin Rosa, and she always made out like if it weren't for her, Cousin Rosa would starve to death because she would be waiting for somebody to come feed her. Cousin Emma had had all kinds of ailments, and Aunt Estelle Drake even said she remembered when Cousin Emma first began to enjoy poor health forty years ago. But I always loved her because she treated me like I was grown and would tell me all sorts of things that Mamma wouldn't, like about people that were stepping out on their wives and husbands and things like that. Cousin Rosa would always say, "Emma, you ought to be ashamed, telling that child all that meanness. There's enough devilment going on in the world without bringing children up on it." But Cousin Emma would say, "Aw, Rosa, don't act a fool. It's the truth, isn't it, and he's got to learn it sometime."

Cousin Emma didn't always do what you asked her to, though. One time I asked her to read to me, and she told me she couldn't read. I couldn't understand why Cousin Rosa hadn't taught her to read like she did her first-grade children, and I worried about it for a long time. When I asked Mamma about it, she said she reckoned Cousin Emma just didn't want to right then; she usually didn't do anything she didn't want to. But I didn't mind, and I used to promise her a lavender dress to wear when I grew up and made a lot of money because I thought it would look pretty with her white hair.

Cousin Emma always made out like it sure was a lot of trouble to get Cousin Rosa off to school every morning, much less do all

the cooking and try to boss all the Negroes she always had working for her. She was always washing woodwork or waxing floors
or something, when she wasn't working outside. Cousin Rosa said,
"Sister has fought dirt all her life." But Cousin Emma would say,
"I've just got to be doing something all the time. Deliver me from
people that have got to sit up in the house and be waited on. I'd
rather be out digging in my flowers in the sunshine than anything
I know."

When Cousin Rosa and Cousin Emma had said enough to each
other, they would both turn around and start in on Auntee if she
was there or maybe even if she wasn't there. But *she* could handle
them all right, and Mamma said she was the *only* person that had
ever been able to. Cousin Rosa and Cousin Emma said Auntee was
just like Cousin Billy Moss; when you went to try to straighten her
out, she would just tell you off and make you like it too.

Cousin Rosa and Cousin Emma were terribly straitlaced about
people's morals, but they couldn't help being crazy about Cousin
Billy because he was always teasing them about all the old bache-
lors and widowers in town. Cousin Billy drank, and sometimes he
gambled. Cousin Rosa and Cousin Emma said that the real trouble
was that he had fallen in with the wrong crowd when he was
growing up down in the Mississippi Bottom. And then he had
married Cousin Effie, who came from Boyd's Landing down on the
river. Her father was a big cotton speculator (Mamma said he just
happened to die at the right time, that was why they had so much
money). But Cousin Emma said Cousin Billy would have been a
thousand times better off if he never had seen that river; and besides, she never could stand old Mrs. Boyd, Cousin Effie's mother,
who played cards *all* the time. Cousin Emma said she thought she
must have died at the bridge table.

The funny thing was that Cousin Emma was a Methodist, like
most of the Mosses, but Cousin Rosa was a Baptist. When I asked
them why this was, Cousin Rosa said she had always gone to the
Baptist Church with Aunt Bessie, her mother. Aunt Bessie had been
a Rogers and she had her own ideas about things. Cousin Emma
went to church just when she felt like it; and, more often than not,
on Sunday morning she would be having the neuralgia or something.

But Cousin Rosa was a big Baptist and went to church every time there was a crack in the church door. She acted like she couldn't ever have been anything but a Baptist for the world; she was always saying she didn't see how a woman could join the church with her husband when she married, if he happened to belong to another church. She used to say, "I've never seen the man yet I'd give up my religion for." But Daddy said she just hadn't seen the man yet and besides it was just the Baptist in her. And even Mamma said, "Those Baptists certainly do stick together. They'll always take up for each other, and they never do let anything unpleasant in their church get any more publicity than they can help." But Daddy said, "It just makes me tired to see Gus Morgan and Tom Maynard and all those other reprobates trotting down the street to the Baptist Church with their Bibles under their arms on Sunday morning when I know perfectly well they've been up all night Saturday night, boozing and gambling down at Johnson's Lake."

And even Cousin Rosa would get a little tired of it all now and then and say, "There certainly are a lot of tacky folks down at the Baptist Church." She never forgot that she could have married one of the Randolphs of Virginia and been an Episcopalian, but she got tired of them always throwing him at her when she went out there to visit, Mamma said, and he was too short for her anyhow.

Cousin Rosa dearly loved society and parties, and Daddy said she would rather greet the guests at the door when you were having a big party than be in Heaven. But Mamma said, "Cousin Rosa would love to entertain every day in the week if somebody else would do all the work. The last time she had the Book Club she was just standing up there in the middle of the dining room floor talking to somebody and holding two plates of ice cream that was melting gently all the while until I just went up and positively took them away from her." But sometimes Cousin Rosa could seem very abrupt, if you didn't know her well, especially on the telephone. Mr. Sam Chism used to say she could hang up a telephone better than anybody he knew, and it was pretty nearly so. When Auntee called her up at school, she would say, "Now, Cousin Rosa, I've got three things to tell you, so don't hang up until I get through." But usually she didn't even say good-by; there would just be a pause, and then down would go the receiver. Blam!

Cousin Emma was a big tease, and she sort of enjoyed taking the wind out of Cousin Rosa's sails when she got so high up in the air. Like she did about Nat that time. Whenever they had trouble with the plumbing, they would send for Nat Halfacre, the Negro plumber and also a big Baptist preacher on the side. The Moss girls were very fond of Nat because he had helped nurse Uncle Forrest when he was sick for so long before he died. Nat would come fix the plumbing any time night or day, but he was always borrowing money from Cousin Rosa. In spite of everything she said, she always let him have it. He usually wanted five dollars; and one day when he had come to borrow some money, they were standing out on the back porch in the hot sunshine. Cousin Rosa was a little provoked with him, and she said, "Goodness, Nat, when I die, you'll be owing me five dollars." Quick as a wink, Cousin Emma rose up from behind the Dorothy Perkins roses, where she was working, and said, "Well, that will be perfectly all right, Rosa, because you're a Baptist and Nat is a Baptist preacher, and he could just come right in and hold the services for you, and we could get our money's worth that way."

But Cousin Rosa wasn't easily downed, even though Cousin Emma worked at it right hard—when she wasn't having a sick headache or arthritis or something. For one thing, Cousin Rosa loved to talk about the Moss family history; but Cousin Emma said she had more live kinfolks than she needed, much less worry about the ones that were dead. One Sunday afternoon when they were taking Miss Eva Kendrick out for a ride in the little blue Ford, they were driving out past Ebenezer Church, which was between the old Moss family cemetery and the road. Cousin Rosa turned around to Miss Eva, who was sitting on the back seat, and said, "Now just as far as you can see around here used to belong to our great-grandfather, Mr. Isaac Moss. Just think of owning all those thousands of acres, and now all we've got is a measly two hundred and fifty!" But as soon as Miss Eva started mirating over all this, Cousin Emma spoke up right quick and said, "Oh, hush, Rosa, if you owned it all every bit right now, you couldn't even pay the taxes on it." And then everybody laughed. Nobody thought Cousin Emma was being hateful; they just knew that was her way with Cousin Rosa.

But the funniest thing that ever happened while they were out riding was out at Fisher's Crossing one hot afternoon in the summertime. They had been out to Miss Clara Vowell's to see about getting some peaches from her. Miss Clara was high as cat's back, but everybody said she had the best peaches in the county—big fat Elbertas and pale Georgia Belles. Anyhow, the girls were driving past the Jordan Methodist Church out at Fisher's Crossing on the way back to town; and Cousin Rosa noticed that a man was up on a ladder painting a sign over the entrance to the cemetery. None of our family was buried there; most of them were down at Mt. Moriah Cemetery out from Barfield. But we all knew Jordan and a lot of the people that were buried there.

All of a sudden Cousin Rosa hollered, "Goodness gracious, he's about to spell 'cemetery' with an 'a'—'c-e-m-e-t-a-r-y.' Stop, Kate, quick, before he goes any further. I've got to tell him to change it. I just can't stand to see something like that done wrong right under your nose." But Cousin Emma said, "Now, Rosa, stop acting like a schoolteacher. Besides, this is a Methodist cemetery; and you're a Baptist and haven't got any right to say anything about what goes on out here. Drive right on, Kate," And so they came on back to town.

Years later I was out at Jordan Church to play for a funeral. The Woodville Methodist Quartet's regular pianist was out of town, and I was filling in for her. After the funeral we got into Mr. Holman's car (he was the tenor) and waited for all the people to go on into the cemetery before we left. We weren't going to the burying because some of the quartet had to get right on back to town. All of a sudden Sally Grigsby, who sang soprano, looked up and said, "Look there, you all, 'cemetery' is spelled wrong right up there on that sign. Wonder how that happened?" And then I spoke up and said, "I can tell you all about it."

7

Amazing Grace

I didn't much want to go with Daddy and Mamma out to Salem Church that Sunday. They were going to have dinner on the ground after preaching, and then after that the Barlow County Singing Convention was going to meet. I was twelve years old, and it looked like to me that I never was going to get away from the country. Every Sunday afternoon we had to go out to Uncle Jim and Aunt Mary's at Maple Grove, where Pa Drake used to live. Pa had been dead for several years, but it looked like Daddy and Mamma didn't know how to quit going. And every time we had to sit around and listen to all those old tales about when the Drake boys were growing up and all the fun they used to have with their neighbors like the Powells and the Sweats.

Pa Drake had come from Virginia after the War and married Grandma, who had been a Sanders, and I think his folks always thought he had married beneath himself. But Daddy used to tell Mamma and she told *me* that they would all have starved to death if it hadn't been for Grandma. Pa had been raised with slaves to wait on him and had gone off to school and learned to read Latin and Greek before he went off to the War, and I reckon he wasn't ever about to learn how to do anything else.

But, anyhow, it looked like everybody in my family was from the country and wasn't ever going to be anywhere else. None of them had ever been off to college because they didn't have any money for *anything,* much less education. They just all went to school out at Maple Grove a few months every year and went to church every Sunday, and that was about as far as any of them got, except Uncle Buford; and he finished high school because Daddy quit school to let him go.

But I was bound and determined that wasn't going to happen to me. I was going to get all the education in the world so I never would have to be ashamed of saying *seen* and *done* and *taken,* and I was going to go places and do things. They needn't to think they were going to keep *me* in Barlow County all my life. I had already had a big argument with Daddy, though, because I said I wanted to go to school at Harvard, which was supposed to be the best school in the whole country. But Daddy said no, sir, I wasn't going to get above my raising and go up there to school with a lot of Yankees that all loved the Negroes so much; I was going to school in the South and like it. It made me mad because I thought he just couldn't stand for me to go off and do things nobody in the whole Drake family had ever done before.

Well, anyhow, somebody in the Salem community had asked us out that Sunday, so about ten o'clock we got in the car and drove off. It was laying-by time, after all the weeds had been chopped out of the cotton, and the cotton was growing like wildfire all along the road. But it was hot as a fox, and I wasn't looking forward to the prospect of eating off the ground with all those ants and worms crawling all over the food and you, too.

It didn't take us long to get out to Salem; it was only about five miles out from Woodville. The church, which was a Baptist church, sat back off the road under some great big oak trees, and people had parked all over the yard without any system at all. They just drove up and stopped wherever they got ready. Most of the cars were old and broken-down looking, and there were a lot of pickup trucks, too. Daddy was always talking about how poor farmers were and what a hard time they had, so I was used to them looking pretty run-down. But what made me kind of tired was the way Daddy seemed to *enjoy* talking about how bad off they were, like there might be something good about having to work so hard and never having any money and never going anywhere and doing anything. For my part, I just couldn't wait to go to New York and see all the museums and theaters and famous people and everything that was going on. But nothing ever happened to any of the Drakes; they just went on year after year as slow as Christmas.

There were still a lot of people in the cars, like couples courting and women nursing babies and changing their diapers right there in your face. But then they began getting out to go in the church, and they were all laughing and hollering like they hadn't seen each other in a thousand years. I thought it was all pretty disgusting and common. It didn't look like any of them had any refinement, and I didn't see how Daddy could be so crazy about them. But he was. He was always talking about some old man out in the country who probably didn't know how to read and write and saying, "He's one of the best men that ever had on a pair of pants"; or he would mention some old woman that was ugly as homemade sin and say, "Yes, I know she's so cross-eyed, when she cries, the tears run down her back, but she's one of the best women you ever saw." That kind of thing worried me because it looked like you had to be ugly and ignorant in order to be good, just like if you really enjoyed something, like going to the picture show, it was probably a bad influence on you. Or at least that was the way a lot of people acted.

The sermon was a pretty regulation Baptist kind with lots of emphasis on whether you were a wise or a foolish virgin and whether you would be ready if Jesus should come tonight. It looked like to me I had more and more things to worry about all the time. It wasn't enough for you to worry about whether or not you were going to get all A's on your report card so you could go to the picture show on school nights and whether you had practiced your hour on the piano every day. Then, on top of all that, you had to worry about going to Heaven and all. It looked like some people just couldn't be satisfied.

So I was pretty glad when church was over and it was time to eat, even if we were going to eat off the ground. The women went on out in the yard and started unloading the food from the cars and spreading their white Sunday tablecloths out under the big oak trees. There was lots of fried chicken and country ham and sliced tomatoes and stuffed eggs and all kinds of cake and pie. And somebody had gone into Woodville right after church to get the ice for the iced tea. Then everybody got a paper plate and started going around and helping himself to everything. When we started around, Mamma whispered to me that we had to take some of everything so as not to hurt anybody's feelings. That was another thing you had to worry about—whether or not you were going to hurt somebody's feelings. But it didn't look like to me anybody was sitting up late at night worrying about whether or not he had hurt *my* feelings.

We went around helping ourselves to everything and trying to eat a little on the side. A cross-eyed woman with buckteeth and dyed hair came up to Mamma and said, "Have you had any of my *cormel* cake?" And Mamma said, "Why, it's Cousin Lucy Belle Sanders, isn't it? No, indeed, I must get some of your caramel cake right away." It seemed like it was always people like that that we had to be kin to, and you always had to be nice to them when you didn't really want to. I used to wonder sometimes whether it would hurt you as much to be nice to people with straight eyes and straight teeth; but then, of course, when they were like that, you didn't have to worry about being *nice* to them in the first place.

Brother Jernigan, the preacher, was stepping around, speaking to all the ladies and eating enough to kill a mule. It looked like I hadn't ever seen a preacher yet that wasn't a big eater and a big man with the ladies; it looked like that just sort of *went* with preaching. And *they* always acted like they had it coming to them just for getting up there once a week and making you wonder about whether or not you were worrying about all the things you should. But they didn't seem to worry much about anything themselves. I reckoned it was sort of like the ravens feeding Elijah or doctors never getting sick or something.

About two o'clock when everybody was full as he could be and all the babies had gone to sleep, everybody began to get up off the ground and brush themselves off and put away the food and everything before the singing convention started. There was going to be a Bette Davis movie on that afternoon at the Dixie Theater in Woodville, and I begged Daddy to let us go on back home so I could see it. But he said, "Now, Robert, we're not going to eat and run like that. That would be just plain ordinary." I didn't like it, but I had to stop and think. It never had occurred to me before that *I* could be ordinary; it was uneducated people out in the country that were ordinary. I didn't exactly know what to make of it, so I followed Mamma and Daddy on into the church without saying anything.

The church was just like an oven, and you could tell that a lot of those people in there weren't any too familiar with soap and water. The place was jam-packed, and there didn't seem to be a breath of air stirring anywhere. The singing convention met only about four times a year, so they were always pretty sure to have a good crowd on hand. People came from all over the county to hear the different solos and quartets and things from every community. Daddy said, though, that they used to meet more often; it was just one more old thing that was dying out.

Everybody got real quiet, and then the Boyd's Landing Quartet got up to sing. They were supposed to be the best quartet in the county; and Daddy said that Mr. Tom Newman, who sang bass, had a voice like distant thunder. They started off with "Alas, and did my Savior bleed?" which was another one of those hymns where you had to low-rate yourself and say you were a worm. ("Would He devote that sacred head for such a worm as I?") It was just like everything else; you never could enjoy anything without thinking maybe you didn't have any right to and were probably going to have to pay for it some day.

I looked at Mamma to see how she was holding out, but she and Daddy were sitting there looking like they couldn't think of anywhere else in the world they would rather be than right there. So I decided I might as well make up my mind to sit there all afternoon, but I sure hoped God was taking notice of how good I was being and was putting it down by my name in the Lamb's Book of Life or wherever He kept all His records.

Finally, after they had sung "Near-o, my God to Thee" (they always pronounced "nearer" that way out in the country) and "On Jordan's stormy banks I stand," they got to "Amazing Grace." That was the first hymn I had ever learned; my nurse, Louella, had taught it to me when I was five years old. And it was written by John Newton, who was a converted slave trader. So I followed right along with the Quartet in my mind.

The first verse went:

Amazing grace! how sweet the sound,
That saved a wretch like me!
I once was lost, but now am found,
Was blind, but now I see.

There you were calling yourself a wretch again, and yet there was supposed to be something sweet about it. I looked around at all those people; and I could see, from the way they looked so far off from the world, so calm and peaceful, that they all thought there was something sweet about being a wretch, too. But why was it so sweet to be a wretch? If it was good to be a wretch, it might also be good to live out in the country and have nothing but lamps for light and have dinner on the ground. Did it mean that maybe God didn't really care whether you said *taken* or got all A's on your report card or lived at Salem or in New York, and that maybe He sort of enjoyed some people saying *taken* and living out in the country, and that maybe He didn't really care whether or not you were worrying about Jesus coming tonight? Was grace maybe something like rain that just fell anyhow and didn't care where it was falling and that was why it was so amazing?

I looked around at Daddy, and his eyes were full—just like they always got whenever he talked about Grandma and Pa or whenever he told me he loved Mamma even more now that he did when they were married or whenever he said he wanted me to have all the opportunities he had never had. Then the Quartet went on to another verse and sang:

'Twas grace that taught my heart to fear,
And grace my fears relieved;
How precious did that grace appear
The hour I first believed!

I was sitting there thinking that grace must be about the most wonderful thing going if it could do all that and that that must have been the way John Newton felt when he wrote that hymn, when, all of a sudden, Daddy put his arm around me and whispered, "Son, you just don't know how much Daddy loves you." And then, right there, in front of all those people, I just reached up and hugged him around the neck.

8

The Summer

of the Window-Peeper

That summer when there was so much carrying-on about the window-peeper in Woodville, I was eight years old; and everybody was saying it was the hottest summer they could ever remember. It looked like, day after day, the sun blazed away at you until by night you were ready to fall into bed from pure exhaustion; but it really didn't get cool enough to go to bed until about midnight. (Aunt Estelle said she just put on her nightgown straight after she got out of the tub without drying off and that was how she stayed cool all night. But Mamma just raised her eyebrows and pursed her lips, and I heard her tell Daddy afterwards that sometimes she positively thought Aunt Estelle didn't have the instincts of a white woman.) Everybody said how badly we needed rain and worried about what would happen to the cotton crop if it didn't come soon.

The first I heard about any window-peeping, though, was one Wednesday when Mamma came home from the Bridge Club (she had belonged to the Wednesday Bridge Club since before the World War; Daddy said sometimes he thought she must have been born with cards in her hand) and told Daddy at the supper table what all the ladies had been talking about.

It seemed that Miss Jo-Ellen Bates that lived out on the edge of town all by herself and said she wasn't afraid of the Devil because he wouldn't have her had been undressing one night to go to bed and, since there weren't any neighbors close around, wasn't too particular about pulling her shades all the way down. All of a sudden, Miss Jo-Ellen heard a man's voice talking to her through the window, asking her to let him come in and calling her "honey" and telling her how much he loved her and "all that kind of rot," Mamma said. Miss Jo-Ellen had been so surprised at first that she said she didn't have her wits about her; but, when she thought about it, it all made her so *mad* that any *man* would be bothering her at her time of life (she was sixty and had waited on her old devil of a father for years until he finally died and then had to put up with two no-good brothers all the time trying to borrow money from her) that she forgot to be scared. Instead, she ran over to the window and started beating on it and hollering, "Get away from here, you low-down son-of-a-bitch." And then of course the shade flew up with a terrible rattle and flapped around the roller, and Miss Jo-Ellen screamed, and whoever it was outside her window took to his heels and left.

Miss Jo-Ellen had tried to pass the whole thing off as a joke, Mamma said, but the Bridge Club "girls," as she always called them, didn't think it was so funny. Of course, everybody knew, Mamma said, that it must have been a colored man because it just wasn't the kind of thing a white man would do. I said why not and, for that matter, what would anybody want to look at Miss Jo-Ellen for, as old and dried-up as she was? But Mamma just said "little pitchers have big ears" and *looked* at Daddy, and I could tell she had a good deal more to say to him after I went to bed.

Well, the summer dragged on without much relief from the heat, and it didn't help matters much when, from time to time, there would be some woman living by herself who would be scared at night by the window-peeper, as everybody began to call him. And it was always the same: he would call them "honey" and all sorts of pet names and beg them to let him come in. He never did try to force his way in, and he never made any threats; so maybe that's why people got more bothered than really worried about it all. But still it made a lot of women uneasy, though the men didn't say much of anything. (Miss Jo-Ellen, though, said she wasn't the least bit "uneasy," if the nasty, stinking thing ever bothered her again, she'd just fill his backside full of buckshot.)

As the summer went on, the window-peeper got bolder and started coming into the middle of town and scaring ladies that weren't living alone, and people began to get really worried about it all. Most of the women took it for granted that the window-peeper was a Negro. (Most of the ladies he had scared had said he *sounded* like one.) And most of them said that it was just one more sign of modern times, how back in the old days when their fathers were alive, no colored man would have dared do such a thing. Their husbands never said much to that, but they began to talk about seeing that the old pistols and shotguns they kept around the house were loaded, and the city police put a couple of extra men on the force until things got "straightened out."

Then one night the window-peeper turned up next door to us and started talking through the screen to Miss Lavonne Matthews that taught the third grade and was going to marry Mr. Billy Hancock that had the Buick agency. It like to have scared her to death, and she said she'd never heard such language in her life, some of the words she didn't even know but she could just *guess* what they meant; it made her blush to the roots of her hair just to think about it. Of course, she ran across the hall right away to her mother and father's room; old Mrs. Matthews immediately rose up, with a whoop, and got out their shotgun and went out the front door in her long white nightgown to find the man. Of course, she never even bothered to wake up Mr. Matthews. She told Mamma she knew she couldn't expect anything from *him* at that hour of the night; it would have taken her fifteen minutes just to get him waked up good, and then before he got out of bed he would have to tell her about his right big toe that was sore, just like he had for every day of the forty-two years they had been married. So she just marched on out the front door in her nightgown with the shotgun under one arm and proceeded on around the house. By that time the man had realized somebody was after him and had gotten away. None of it fazed Mrs. Matthews, though; when she was telling Mamma about it, she said, "And it's a good thing I didn't meet him because I'd-a shot him as sure as anything in the world." And Mamma said yes, she knew Mrs. Matthews would have, but the thing for them to do now was to put their heads together and lay a trap for the window-peeper because obviously (and here Mamma looked at Mrs. Matthews over my head), he was coming back to peep at Miss Lavonne again.

But before they got their plans laid good, something happened that got things even more mixed up. One stifling hot afternoon, Mrs. Virgil Hays that lived across the street came running in our front door with her tongue hanging out and said, like it was something she was really proud of having done, "Well, I've just seen our window-peeper! I know that Negro must be the one because I've seen him hanging around here out under the street-light in the late afternoons, not doing anything much but looking around, and now I've just this minute seen him go in Miss Eva Kendrick's back door!"

Of course, Mamma didn't do a thing but step to the telephone and call Miss Eva down the street. Miss Eva was always as thick as thieves with the Negroes; she lent them money at ten per cent and was always having business dealings with them, even seeing them in her kitchen late at night until everybody said she was going to get knocked in the head by one of them if she didn't watch out. Well, when Mamma got her on the telephone, Miss Eva said the only colored man to come to her house that afternoon was John Alfred Washburn and he was her cook's son and going to the state college for Negroes and she could vouch for him. And then she proceeded to turn around and tell John Alfred, who was standing right there, that Mamma thought he was the window-peeper and wasn't that funny, with him being a "college boy"? And it scared Mamma and made her so mad that she just hung up in Miss Eva's face.

Well, Mamma and old Mrs. Matthews got their trap set for the window-peeper as soon as they could. One of the night watchmen on the city force was to be hiding behind the big hydrangea bushes by Miss Lavonne's window, and there was to be a dummy fixed up to look like Miss Lavonne in her bed. Everything was ready, and then of course old Mr. Alec Sides, the watchman, went to sleep sitting in his split-bottom chair behind the hydrangea bushes and didn't wake up until he heard the window-peeper talking through Miss Lavonne's window, calling her "honey" and "darling" and begging her to let him come in. Mr. Sides hollered and ordered the man to stay where he was, but he ran; and, when Mr. Sides, who weighed two hundred and fifty pounds, started after him, he tripped and fell over a tree root. The shotgun went off and sprayed the window-peeper across the back, but he got away.

Mamma had already told Mrs. Matthews her suspicions about John Alfred Washburn, so the next day the officers didn't do a thing but call on him at home. They found him washing a bloody shirt (he said he had cut himself), so they just made him take off the shirt he had on; and, sure enough, there was Mr. Sides' buckshot streaked across his back.

Well, that was all the evidence the officers said they needed for a conviction, and so John Alfred was sentenced to two years in the state penitentiary and ordered not to ever set foot in Woodville again when he got out. And so most people began to breathe easy again—that is, all of them except Miss Eva Kendrick, who went to the judge and told him John Alfred was her cook's son and in college and wouldn't have dreamed of doing anything like that and they must have made a mistake. Of course, the judge and officers didn't pay any attention to her and, besides, they all knew what a nigger-lover she was. But it made Mamma perfectly furious when she heard about it; that was twice, she said, when Miss Eva had betrayed her own people. And, as for herself, Mamma said she would always live in fear that John Alfred would come back to Woodville someday.

And so the summer finally came to an end, and it rained, and the cotton crop turned out all right after all. But Miss Lavonne Matthews broke off her engagement to Mr. Billy Hancock and got sick and finally had a nervous breakdown. They said she would cry and wring her hands and say she couldn't bear to give herself in marriage to Mr. Billy now that she had been "defiled" by all those words John Alfred had called her through the window. But Mamma said thunderation, that was all a young girl's foolishness and any God-fearing white woman ought to be nothing but glad that John Alfred was shut up now where he couldn't ever look at or talk to one of them like that again and she was sorry only that he hadn't been put there for life.

But finally all the to-do about the window-peeper died down; after a while, people began to talk less and less about him and turn their attention to something else. There always was plenty to talk about in Woodville anyway. But, every now and then, I used to think about John Alfred all shut up there in the state penitentiary and wonder whether, in spite of all his college education, he was thinking about the white ladies in Woodville as much as they still thought about him. And I wondered whether he ever really thought, when he used to call them all those names and beg them to let him come in, that they ever really would let him. And I wondered, if they had, whether he would have been pleased or disappointed with what he found there.

9

The Bridegroom Cometh

When I was eleven years old, my cousin, Stuart, was married to Martha Claiborne from Dawson, Kentucky. Her father, who was dead, had been a big lawyer, and her mother had been a Louisville belle. But the thing was, they were Presbyterians. I always wondered how the Drakes ever managed to reconcile themselves to that; after all, Uncle John, Stuart's father, was a Methodist preacher, and the Drakes were all Methodists from the tops of their heads to the soles of their feet. But nobody said anything except Martha seemed awfully sweet and her mother must have been pretty when she was younger.

I had always been crazy about Stuart because he was so fine and upstanding and knew exactly what he wanted to do and never seemed afraid of anything, and I wanted to be exactly like him when I grew up. He was tall and blond and handsome, and I used to wish he was my older brother because he was exactly the kind of older brother I would have picked out myself.

Well, it was during the war, and Stuart and Martha were going to marry right after he got his second lieutenant's wings. And I was going with Uncle Buford and Aunt Janie to the wedding up in Dawson. (Daddy said he didn't want to have to get dressed up like a country corpse and stand around and "ooh" and "aah" to a lot of strange people—and besides you couldn't trust Kentuckians anyhow, they might be Republicans. But Mamma said it was just a sign he was getting old.) But I was very excited because I had always like weddings. They were so grand because everybody was all dressed up, with flowers and candles all around. And then a wedding seemed to sort of *mean* something, and I always liked anything that did that—even funerals. Because it looked like so much of life didn't seem to *mean* anything: you just got up and went to school or wherever you worked and then came home and went to bed and then did it all over again the next day. But at a wedding or a funeral or a graduation or an election you could sort of see the *meaning* of whatever was going on even if you didn't exactly know what it was. So I was all excited because it seemed like Stuart and Martha were going to be part of something that *meant,* and I thought that was fine. And they seemed terribly in love, and I thought that maybe they really had been made for each other, like the stories in the *Ladies' Home Journal* always said.

I had heard Mamma say the Claibornes were supposed to have money, so I wasn't surprised when we drove up to their house and it was very impressive, with a great big yard and a high wall around it. Everybody was in a big hurry to get to the church, so I didn't have much time to look around. We changed into our wedding clothes upstairs, and then we were off.

You could certainly tell the Claibornes were what everybody always called "socially prominent" because the church was full of women in high-style clothes, and a lot of the men had on tuxedos. But we just marched right on in in our regular Sunday clothes and sat right down in front on the groom's side of the church where everybody would know that we were Stuart's folks. I was almost ashamed of the way we looked; it was almost like we weren't doing right by Stuart and Martha. But it didn't seem to bother the Drakes any; they always acted like blood was more important than money, even if most of the world didn't think so these days.

The organist was playing a lot of sad, sweet music like "Lie-bestraüm" and "I Love You Truly" while the ushers were lighting the candles. They were most of them not Dawson boys but brought-on fellows, as Daddy would say—boys that Martha had gone with at college before she met Stuart. She had had lots of beaux, and everybody said Stuart was mighty lucky to get her. Some of the ushers were sort of shaky while they were lighting the candles, and I imagined they might have had a drink or two already. But what really made me mad was when some fool man stood up to sing, and he was almost swaying in time to the music. And Aunt Janie got tickled because, being a singer herself, she knew the music; when he got to "Oh Promise Me," he put in that part about "those first sweet violets of early spring" at least three times. It almost made me sick, though. Everything was so wonderful for Stuart and Martha, and he had to go and spoil it all by acting that way. That was just what you got when you went to bringing in people from out of town for things.

Then the wedding march started, and the procession began coming in. Stuart and one of his air force friends, who was the best man, came out of the vestibule; I thought he was the grandest looking thing I had ever seen—almost like King Arthur in an army air force uniform instead of shining armor. But Stuart wasn't looking at any of us; he was looking up the aisle for Martha. And when she came by us, she was the most beautiful thing you ever saw. She had on a white satin dress with a long veil and train, and then over her face she had the thinnest kind of short veil. I had read somewhere that that was because the bride was supposed to be too shy to face everybody until she was a married woman; but I didn't think Martha would be afraid to face anybody, any time, she was so beautiful—and she *had* Stuart.

Then Uncle John, who was all dressed up in his ankle-beater— which was what Daddy always called a frock coat, just for meanness—performed the ceremony. And after he had pronounced them man and wife, the maid of honor lifted up Martha's face veil; and Stuart kissed her right there in front of everybody. I thought that was the most exciting part of all, though I could tell the Drakes didn't especially like it. They were always terribly dignified in public.

When we got back to Martha's house for the reception, there were so many people all laughing and talking that you could hardly hear yourself think. And they all introduced me as "Robert, Jr.," which made me feel like I was a baby instead of almost twelve.

And then after everybody had been through the receiving line and they had taken pictures and pictures, Stuart and Martha went upstairs to get ready to go away. But just before they did, they posed for just one more picture on the stairs. Stuart bent down and looked into Martha's face, and I thought I had never seen anybody look the way they did before. And I felt almost embarrassed and like I had intruded on their privacy. It was like they belonged to each other so completely, they didn't even have to talk; they just understood each other without saying a word. And it made you think about what it said in the wedding ceremony about marriage being like Christ and His Church and about what the Bible said about the twain being one flesh. Then they turned and ran up the stairs; and, all of a sudden, I wished I could go off with them and be *theirs* somehow and catch some of the love that was running over from them, they had so much of it. There was a lump in my throat, and tears came in my eyes, and I turned away so nobody could see me. It was sort of like at the movies when you wished you could go off right then and live in New York or Paris and do all sorts of wonderful things, too, but next morning you had to go right on back to school and learn some more of the products of the Great Plains states. You knew that was the way it had to be, but you still got worked up about something you couldn't have; it looked like you just did it to spite yourself, almost.

For three years Stuart and Martha moved all over the country, but every now and then they would breeze in down home for a day or two. And then we would all go out to Uncle John and Aunt Estelle's and listen to them tell about where all they had been and what they had been doing. Martha was able to go with him every time he was moved to another base, but we all knew it probably wouldn't be long before Stuart was sent overseas. And, finally, when he and Martha were out in California, he got his orders to go. Martha came on back to her mother's, but every now and then she would come down to see all of us and read us Stuart's letters, though he wasn't able to say much because of the censorship and all.

And then one day almost a month after the war had ended and I was in high school, the telephone rang. It was Martha; she had gotten a telegram that Stuart had been killed in a plane crash in Burma, when the war was already over. And then for a while it was just awful. We went out to Uncle John's, and Aunt Estelle was beside herself, and people were coming in and out of the house. But I didn't want to see anybody or talk to them; I wanted to get off by myself where I could think about Stuart and Martha and see what it all *meant*. When anybody died, you had to get busy and make the world all over *without* them and then think about it over and over so it wouldn't hurt so bad every time you thought about them. But, in a way, it was almost like I had expected it to happen, like Stuart and Martha had so much love that it couldn't go on that way. And the most terrible thing was that there couldn't even be a funeral; it just went on and on. When there was a funeral for anybody, it at least meant that everything was over and you could sort of put everything straight in your mind. But now we just had to go on and on. There was something terrible and almost embarrassing about it—like the curtain not coming down at the end of a play.

Finally, the government sent word that they had buried Stuart over in Burma, and that helped some. Everything sort of got back to normal, but I couldn't get Stuart adjusted in my mind. It was almost like I was afraid I might get *used* to him being dead, and I had loved him so much, I couldn't bear to do that. *Somebody* had to keep thinking about him, and it didn't seem right for everybody just to go right on like he hadn't ever existed.

But little by little, everybody did begin to settle down again, in spite of everything. Martha still came down to see us, but it wasn't the same any more. And I thought I could tell that she was having to put up an effort to keep coming, and then one night I heard Daddy tell Mamma he wouldn't be a bit surprised if Martha wasn't beginning to set out. And Mamma said well, maybe she ought to; she was still a young woman. But surely she couldn't do that, as much as she had loved Stuart. How *could* Mamma and Daddy talk like that? But I think I already knew then that they were probably right and that Martha ought to marry again. And, in a way, I was expecting her to.

Then the last year I was in high school, the government sent word all of a sudden that they were sending Stuart's body back home. There we were with everybody maybe having got used to him being gone, and now we had to go through it all again. Even I, in spite of everything I had thought, had gotten almost used to it; but now it just brought the whole thing back and made it almost worse than ever. In a way, it all seemed sort of unfair—maybe because it made me feel like I hadn't held on to Stuart in my mind as much as I should, that I really had gotten used to him being dead.

Well, they were going to have a big funeral for Stuart up in Dawson because he was the first soldier to be brought back there, and we all went up. When we got to Martha's house, there were a lot of people there all talking like they were almost at a party or a wedding instead of a funeral. And Martha asked Mamma if she thought it would be all right for her to wear the brown flowered silk she had on, black was so depressing. And I didn't know what to think. How could she say that, when Stuart was right there in a steel casket, with a flag on top, in front of the big fireplace? Then I looked at Martha going up the stairs to get her hat before we left for the church, and I remembered how Stuart had looked at her when they were standing on the stairs that day at the wedding reception, and I wanted to cry. But then when she was halfway up the stairs, she turned around all of a sudden and looked back at the casket a long time, like she was determined to fix it in her mind forever. And then, all in a minute, she turned back around and flew up the steps; and then I heard a door slam.

Everybody was talking louder than ever, but I just stood there by the stairs thinking about Stuart and Martha and wishing I could cry forever and ever because I had loved them so much and maybe all that love of theirs and mine didn't *mean* anything and I had gotten so it maybe didn't matter any more and I was ashamed. And then, from upstairs, over all the talking, I heard the sound of crying. It wasn't like when you are just disappointed and you feel sorry for yourself and want to make everybody else sorry for you. But it was like when the whole world has come to an end for you and you know you don't have anything left to hold on to and you want to be dead and out of it all. And it sounded final and terrible, and I thought about Rachel that would *not* be comforted. And then—I didn't know exactly why—I began to feel a lot better.

10

Aunt Janie

and the Angels

Aunt Janie was Uncle Buford's wife, but before that she had been Jane Malone. But everybody in Woodville called her Janie. She taught in the grammar school for years and years and directed the Methodist Choir on the side. Daddy said she had tried to quit the choir a couple of times, but they just wouldn't let her. He said they just positively *drafted* her.

Because she was so faithful and everybody loved her so much. You could call her up and say there was somebody you never heard of going to be buried out at Haley's Switch that afternoon and they didn't have anybody to sing; and she would say, "I'll go," every time. I think Uncle Buford wanted her to kind of slow down and not do so much of that, but it looked like she just couldn't do it. Mamma said, "Jane just lives on excitement"; and, in a way, it was true because she just had to be doing something. If she wasn't teaching school or singing, she was going to see somebody sick or taking somebody out riding that was a shut-in or something.

But where I loved her best was at weddings because there just wasn't anybody that could sing those old wedding songs that you had heard a thousand times the way she could: things like "Because" and "Calm as the Night." It was like she was always tickled to death for the bride and groom and so happy that she just sort of ran over into the music. And one thing was sure: you could always understand every word she sang. (It was certainly different from Miss Ora Pearl Henderson that old Mr. Oscar Campbell said he never understood but one thing she sang and that was "Jesus Christ" and he could run a mile while she was singing that.) And then, of course, every year Aunt Janie had to put on the Christmas pageant at the church. One year we had a White Christmas with a great big Christmas tree all dusted over with lime (I never had seen a *real* White Christmas with snow), and the choir sang "We Three Kings of Orient Are" while the Wise Men came in bringing gifts to the Baby Jesus.

I reckon Aunt Janie might have really done something with her voice if she had tried, maybe even made a career of it. But she never seemed to feel like she ought to have been off singing somewhere else. She was so wild about Uncle Buford, and everybody in Woodville loved her so much.

The bad part was that she and Uncle Buford didn't have any children, and I used to wonder if she was ever sorry about it. But I guessed maybe she just didn't have time to think about it, she was so busy teaching and singing. And then, of course, she wasn't really well. She had had diabetes for years and had to take an insulin shot every morning of the world. And she was always having to weigh her food and buy special kinds of candy and cake in Memphis, but you never heard her say a word about it. It was just sort of part of her, and you just didn't think anything about it. But one time I heard Mamma tell somebody that Aunt Janie said she wondered if it was all worth the trouble, and that sort of made me think. It never had occurred to me that maybe Aunt Janie ever got *tired* of taking insulin and dieting any more than she did of teaching and singing. She never said a word about not feeling well or anything.

The year I was in the eighth grade Aunt Janie was busy running around getting ready for the Christmas pageant, but I didn't like the dark circles that had been coming under her eyes lately. But it looked like the tireder she looked, the more energy she had. Maybe Mamma was right and Aunt Janie was really living on excitement; it didn't seem like she could bear not being mixed up in things. Or maybe it wasn't really excitement that Aunt Janie lived on as much as love. Maybe she had so much love running over that she just had to have somebody to spill it over on, or something like that.

Anyhow, the Sunday before Christmas she put on the Christmas pageant with a manger scene right in front of the pulpit. The choir was all dressed up in white robes, and they really raised the roof when they let out on "Joy to the World," which was the last song, with Aunt Janie leading away for dear life. Then a couple of days before Christmas Aunt Janie said she had to go to Memphis to do some last-minute Christmas shopping. Uncle Buford didn't much want her to go; she was going to have all the Drakes over for Christmas dinner and she was already worn out from getting ready for that. But he didn't say anything; you couldn't say anything to Aunt Janie, anyway, when she had her mind on doing something for other folks.

Well, when she got back from Memphis, she was feeling pretty bad, and on Christmas Eve morning she just couldn't get out of bed. The turkey was already in the roaster for the dinner, but Uncle Buford just stepped in and called it off. I knew from that she must be feeling mighty bad, but I didn't think too much about it until the doctor decided maybe, on account of the diabetes, they had better take her to the hospital in Memphis. So on Christmas morning they took her to Memphis, and by the time they got there she was in a diabetic coma.

I knew Mamma and Daddy were worried because they said the diabetes had lowered her resistance and made it harder for her to fight off anything else. But I thought maybe it wasn't that as much as she was worn out from singing and teaching and loving people so much. Nobody in our family had died since Pa Drake, and that had been when I was little. And now the possibility that Aunt Janie might die just knocked the props out from under me. Death was always exciting, and I had often thought that maybe there was something interesting about walking down the aisle behind the casket and sitting down in front where everybody could see you. But not now--not because of Aunt Janie.

When I heard how sick she was, I felt like she wasn't maybe going to get well. It was like she had loved too much, maybe even loved herself to death; and, when the pneumonia came along, she just didn't have anything to fight it with. There was snow and ice on the roads, so we couldn't get to Memphis; we just had to sit there waiting for the phone to ring, feeling her slipping farther away from us all the time.

Early Monday morning Uncle Buford called to say that it was all over. I just couldn't get over it. Even though I had maybe been expecting her to die, I couldn't believe I never would hear her sing any more or hear her tell Fannie to put my name in the pot because I was going to stay for supper. It was just like one part of my life had been blacked out.

I couldn't bear to go over to Uncle Buford's when they got back from Memphis, and I didn't want to see Aunt Janie lying in a casket and hear everybody talk about how natural she looked when she was dead. Daddy was over there nearly all the time because Uncle Buford was his baby brother and he couldn't bear to leave him alone now. So when I woke up crying in the night, Mamma didn't know what to do. She said, "Would you like to go over and be with Uncle Buford?" But I said, "No, I don't ever want to go back over there. It'll never be the same without Aunt Janie." And Mamma said, "Oh, yes, you will. We just have to get used to these things because that's the way life is. Now you just go right on and get ready to go to the funeral tomorrow because we can't ever just quit."

I knew she was probably right. You just couldn't stop; you had to go on— somewhere, wherever it was you thought you were going. So the next morning I went with Daddy back over to Uncle Buford's. Everybody was going in to look at Aunt Janie one more time before they closed the casket, but I didn't. I wanted always to remember her like she was, singing "Joy to the World" that last time.

When we got to the church, I went in with my cousin Lina, but I didn't think about it being exciting to be mixed up with a funeral any more, and I could hardly see who all was there for the tears. And, as we sat down and I looked around, I began to wonder who would be next after Aunt Janie. Some of the family certainly didn't look as spry as they used to. Maybe I was just *started* going to funerals, and I didn't see how I could stand it, and I hugged Lina close.

But then the choir got up to sing; they were all there with their white robes on and Annie Mae Lipscomb was at the organ. They sang "How Firm a Foundation," and I was glad because Aunt Janie wouldn't have wanted any real sad music at her funeral. They got to the verse that went:

When through the deep waters I call thee to go,
The rivers of woe shall not thee overflow;
For I will be with thee, thy troubles to bless
And sanctify to thee thy deepest distress.

Well, I felt like I was in pretty deep water now, and I sure hoped God really meant that thing.

Then Brother Wiley got up and stood right where Aunt Janie had when she led the choir at the Christmas program. He was standing right where the winter sun was shining in through the big west window with Christ ascending into Heaven and angels all around, and he seemed to look more up into the sunlight than at us. He just stood there for a minute without saying anything, and I could see there were tears in his eyes.

And then finally he said, "Friends, this is a sad duty for all of us; it was hard for the choir to sing and hard for Annie Mae to play. And yet we knew we couldn't let Janie down; she never let anybody down herself. I can't say much; most of you knew her a lot longer than I did. And yet in the few years that I was with her, I don't think I ever saw her too tired or too concerned with her own life to think of somebody else. She just couldn't operate any other way. And I like to think that she is still serving and loving in Heaven. Last week she stood here and sang 'Joy to the World,' and now maybe somewhere up in Heaven, Janie is singing with the angels."

Then he sat down, and the choir started in on "My Faith Looks Up to Thee." I sat there and thought about what Brother Wiley had said. I knew now, maybe for the first time, that when part of your life goes out, you just have to get busy and fill it in right quick; thinking about the emptiness doesn't do you any good at all. Maybe, in a way, that's what Aunt Janie had been afraid of always—emptiness and not meaning anything to all the people around her. Now there were plenty of things for me to do: Uncle Buford needed me to love him, for one thing. Maybe even if I had lost Aunt Janie in one way, I had hold of her forever in another way because maybe now her love was working in me and through me, still trying to reach out to other people, still trying to keep from being empty. I looked up into the light that was streaming down around the pulpit, and it was almost like I could hear Aunt Janie singing "Joy to the World" all over again—only this time with the angels.

11

Mrs. Higgins' Heart

Mrs. Higgins was a little old woman who wore her hair in a knot on top of her head, and she lived in the big red brick house up on the corner from us. She had an old-maid daughter named Willie, who was named for her father, Mr. William Magruder Higgins, who had been a druggist; and she had a little spitz dog named Wallie, who was named for the Duchess of Windsor. Mrs. Higgins took boarders for years and years (Mamma used to board with her before she and Daddy were married), but finally one day she just got tired of it all and quit. When people asked her who was living with her now and what she was giving them to eat, she would say, "I'm not cooking for anybody but me and Willie, and I don't do that except when I get ready."

People thought she was a little hard on Willie sometimes because Willie had never gotten away from home and married. Instead, she had always stayed right there and helped her mother with the boarding house, and she also made cakes for people on the side. Mamma said she had never seen prettier wedding cakes than the ones Willie made. And it was true, too. They always had the most delicate roses and leaves and ropes made out of icing on them, and sometimes instead of the bride and groom on top she would put a little glass full of lilies of the valley and then ice it all around so the lilies of the valley looked like they were growing out of the top of the cake. But Mamma thought her everyday cakes weren't so good. She said, "You can't make a cake out of water and margarine and expect it to stand up." Once Mrs. Higgins even said to Mamma, "Lucille, you can make better cakes than Willie, but you can't decorate them," but when Mamma got home, she said, "Well,

I've never *tried* decorating them."

Willie didn't seem to mind staying at home and never getting married so much; she always seemed to stay busy doing something. She used to paint china as well as make cakes. She had learned how to paint when she went off to Ward's Seminary in Nashville as a young girl, and she still had a lot of her work around the house—pitchers and cake plates and things like that. One time Lois Edwards, Mrs. Higgins' niece that they took to raise when her mother died, said, "You know, Willie sneaked around the house and scratched all the dates off that china she painted at Ward's so folks wouldn't know how old she was." And Mrs. Higgins said she had forgotten exactly when Willie was born herself, so she wasn't sure just how old she was. But Willie didn't seem to *worry* about getting old. She just went right on making cakes and trying to hold Mrs. Higgins down whenever she got all worked up about something.

And Mrs. Higgins was always worked up about *something*. Sometimes it was the kinfolks, and goodness knows there were enough of them. Her mother had been a Marshall, and that made her kin to just about half the county, especially all the people out at Winbush and Tabernacle. And then sometimes she got started on her kinfolks over in Monroe County, and that was really something.

One of her best tales was about the time they tried to break Cousin Susie Anderson's will (we were kin to her, too, but on the other side of the house). It seemed that Cousin Jack, Cousin Susie's oldest son, was trying to get all her property because he said he had taken care of her in her last illness and deserved to have it. But Cousin Maud, his sister, said she knew what he was up to and she was going to have Cousin Susie's will broken. So there was a big lawsuit, and they got Mrs. Higgins over there to testify about whether or not Cousin Susie had been of sound mind in her last days or something like that. But they didn't want her to hear a certain part of the testimony; so they shut her up in a little room with Mr. Horace Bridges, the Monroeville undertaker, and old Miss Edmonia Wilkes from home, who were witnesses too. Mrs. Higgins would laugh and say, "Yes, sir, there we were locked up in that little room; and poor old Mrs. Wilkes had taken a dose of salts that morning and she was perfectly miserable." When I told Mamma about it, she laughed and said, "That sounds like Miss Edmonia all right. I never knew her to start off to go anywhere that she didn't have to run back and take a dose of salts or an enema before she left." It seemed like Miss Edmonia was one of those people who took an enema every other day just on principle.

Anyhow, Cousin Maud got the will broken, and Brother Jack didn't get to put that one over. He had always wanted to get all the money in the family, she said. He used to say he thought things ought to be like they were in England, where the oldest son got all the money. But he never would get by *her*. When their father, Cousin Matthew, died, he made Cousin Maud the executrix of his estate; and that like to have surprised Cousin Jack to death. She said he collapsed and fainted on the streets of Monroeville when he heard about it. Anyhow, it wasn't too long after Cousin Susie's will was broken that Cousin Jack died himself, but Cousin Maud never had any time for him dead or alive. She used to say, "He wasn't obedient to his parents when he was young, and he was the most selfish man in the world when he got grown, and he's burning in Hell for it right now, too." It used to just kill Daddy to hear her talk that way; he couldn't imagine anybody not getting along with their own flesh and blood.

But Mrs. Higgins would talk about her kinfolks any way she pleased, just like Cousin Maud, and she would probably agree with anything you said about them, too. And when she wasn't talking about the kinfolks, she was lambasting the Negroes that worked for her. They used to try her soul because they were so lazy and she had so much energy. She would say, "I got that nasty stinking nigger John working in my garden, and I've got to stay right on his back all the time to get any work out of him, and then I might as well do it myself. The niggers these days just aren't worth the spit it would take to drown them." But we knew she didn't really mean half the things she said, and all the Negroes liked to work for her.

Because she had the kindest heart in the world. Mamma said, "If you were sick in bed and didn't have anybody to cook or wash for you, Mrs. Higgins would come in and do it all and anything else that needed to be done. And there aren't many people this day and time that would do that. She's got the kindest heart in the world." But Cousin Rosa and Cousin Emma Moss didn't feel that way about her. They said she had the most terrible temper in the world and would just as soon lay you out as not. But Mamma said, "Cousin Rosa and Cousin Emma can never forgive her for what she said about Cousin Jack Moss' wife when he got married. They didn't marry until late in life, and Mrs. Higgins said Mary Sue was so old-maidish she was probably still wearing high-bust corsets."

It was true that Mrs. Higgins had a bad temper, but most of the time she kept it under control. Mamma said, "Mrs. Higgins hasn't got a bit of sense in the world when she gets mad. She just flies off the handle and lays you out and then forgets all about it and expects you to do the same." I never had seen her mad, but I didn't imagine she was as bad as that woman over in Boone County that Cousin Emma Moss used to tell about that had such an awful temper. This old woman and her husband were always fighting like cats and dogs, and she would make the most terrible threats if she got mad enough. One day they had a big argument out on the back porch by the old covered cistern; and she said, "O, you just make me so mad, I've got a good notion to jump right in this cistern." The old man must have been pretty tired of all her carrying on because he just jerked off the top of the cistern and said, "Hit the bottom!" And she jumped right in. And then he had to get a rope and get her out. And he said that if she had drowned, he never would have told a soul because they would have all sworn he pushed her in. But it was a dry year, and there wasn't much water in the cistern.

Mrs. Higgins never did go that far, but I did hear what she told old Mr. Conner who lived across the street from her. His wife had just died, and I guess he was lonely because he was always coming over to see Mrs. Higgins and Willie. One time she was telling Mamma all about it; and she said, "Lucille, I know that old fool is lonesome, but I haven't got time to worry with him. His wife was the best woman in the world; she was so good I bet she never even chewed gum. But that old devil would try the patience of Job, and I reckon that's what helped put her in her grave. Now, any time he can, he comes over here to talk to us. Just as sure as he sees the light go on in this living room at night. And in the daytime he comes pussyfooting over her with food for my chickens, and most of it isn't anything but coffee grounds. The other day I looked out the window when he was going back to the hen-house and said, 'Mr. Conner, my chickens won't lay on coffee grounds.' But he keeps coming just the same. But the other day he really capped the climax. He came over here about ten o'clock in the morning, and it was hot as the mischief, and there Willie and I were back in the kitchen working like two niggers trying to get some watermelon rind pickle put up before it got so hot up in the day. And Mr. Conner came sashaying back in the kitchen and said, real pitiful, 'I've got two bushels of peaches over home that need to be put up, and I wonder if you could give me a hand with them.' And I said, 'Hell, no!'" And then she looked over her glasses at Mamma, and I thought she looked just like a setting hen that was going to cackle. And then she said, "Now, Lucille, I am not a cursing woman, but that old fool made me so damned mad I didn't know what else to say."

But Mrs. Higgins could see a joke in a minute, even when it was on her. Like the time years ago when she had her teeth out. Mr. Higgins had died, and they were living in Memphis. She decided to start having her teeth out, so she got Mr. Higgins' nephew, who lived down there, to go down town with her to a big high-priced dentist that didn't do anything but take out teeth. She said she didn't know how many he was going to take out the first time, but she didn't think but two or three. The dentist was going to give her some gas to put her to sleep, and Mr. Higgins' nephew was standing right there by the chair. She said, "There I was helpless as a baby and going under the influence of the anesthetic, and Mr. Higgins' nephew spoke up and said, 'How many are you going to take out, doctor?' And that fool doctor said, 'I'm going to make a clean sweep.' And when I woke up, I didn't have a tooth in my head." And then she would die laughing.

Well, time went along, and she and Willie kept on doing mostly what they wanted to. Willie kept on making cakes, and Mrs. Higgins kept on washing up after her and talking night and day. They just sort of took things easy and didn't let anything bother them. Like the business about the poinsettias. Willie had some real pretty poinsettias in the dining room that bloomed almost every Christmas, and everybody that walked along the street said how pretty they were. But when they wouldn't bloom for Christmas, Willie would just put artificial blooms on the plants, and most people never knew the difference until Miss Ernestine Crowder went over to carry on over them the way she always did about everything.

She said, "Oh, dear, they look just like velvet and feel like it, too. Why, I declare, they *are* velvet." But Mrs. Higgins and Willie didn't care as long as people thought they were pretty.

And then one morning when I was in high school, Mrs. Higgins had a heart attack. They thought for a while that she was a goner. But she just showed *them*. The doctor said he had never seen a heart with such come-back in his life. And soon she began to get better. But Aunt Lulie, Mrs. Higgins' younger sister, came from over in Arkansas to help take care of her and almost drove Willie crazy. Aunt Lulie was seventy-four years old, and she thought nothing of getting up on the dining-room table and washing the big stained-glass light shade with all the grapes on it. And then she would talk to Mrs. Higgins and get her all excited. Mrs. Higgins was supposed to stay very quiet and not do any more talking than she could help, but everybody knew she would just as soon be dead as be in a fix like that. And Mamma said maybe it would be better for her to *be* dead in that case. But Mrs. Higgins kept on talking just the same. When Willie and Aunt Lulie had gone out of the room and left you alone with her, she would look at you and grin and say, "Let's talk. They won't know anything about it."

She got better and was able to be up and around the house and sit out on the porch and talk to everybody that went by. Sometimes she would even wash the dishes and fix the vegetables for dinner, when Willie would let her. And she kept right on talking all the time. But then she would overtax her strength and have a relapse. Finally, after I went away to college, she kept getting weaker and weaker until she was nearly always in bed. And she didn't seem to get up in the air about things like she used to. The last time I saw her was at Christmastime; I sat with her while the others were eating Christmas dinner. Lois Edwards was home from Memphis, where she had a job, and she told Mamma she almost wished Mrs. Higgins would go on and die because she was getting so feeble and so unlike her old self. Sometimes she would wake up in the night and cry; and Willie, who slept right across the room, would get up and say, "What's the matter, Mamma? What do you want?" And Mrs. Higgins would say, "I just want people to quit fighting and killing each other. I just want peace in this world."

Two days after Christmas our telephone rang real early in the morning before we had gotten up. It was Lois and she said Mrs.

Higgins had had another heart attack and died very early that morning. Mamma went over to Daddy's bed and said, "Daddy, Mrs. Higgins has just died. I've got to run up to Willie's right away and see if there's anything I can do." Daddy was still about half asleep, but he rolled over and looked up at Mamma a long time like he couldn't take in exactly what she was saying. And then he said, "Well, bless her old soul. She had a heart in her as big as a mule."

12

Mrs. Edney

and the Person

from Porlock

Mrs. Edney was my English teacher when I got to the last two years of high school. Everybody had always told me what fun she was, but they also said she could be very sarcastic, too, if you didn't work or tried to talk back to her. So I was going to try to work hard and not rub her the wrong way.

Mrs. Edney used to be Vada Hobson from out at Louisa before she married, and most of her friends still called her "Hob." But she had been married to Mr. Gene Edney for ever since I could remember. He wasn't a well man, and I always thought myself he looked pretty much like a "haunt" must look—real thin with piercing cold blue eyes. And he coughed a lot, which made some people say he had consumption. But everybody said Mrs. Edney was crazy about him. Anyhow, she wasn't broken out with good looks herself. She was about five and a half feet tall and didn't weigh much more than a hundred pounds. Practically all her hair was gone, so she had to arrange what few strands she had as carefully as she could to make it look like she had more. This made her have a real high forehead, and somehow she always looked like she was waiting for you to answer a question she had asked you. But she always made a joke about not having much hair; sometimes she called herself the surrey with the fringe on top.

A lot of people thought maybe she was trying to rise above her beginnings—being from out at Louisa and all. But it seemed to me she was always telling us about something that happened out there a long time ago—like about the time the Jamieson boys all got on a big drunk and started for the graveyard to dig up their old father to give him a drink, the liquor was so good. I never for a minute thought she wanted to go *back* there, but she was glad she was *from* there.

The first thing you noticed about Mrs. Edney as a teacher was that she didn't seem to have much system. Her desk was completely covered with books, and she always had to hunt for about five minutes to find her text before she could start class. And she didn't seem to have any set time for assigning themes and quizzes; she just sort of did it on the spur of the moment. What seemed to matter more than anything else was making you like what you were reading as much as she did.

But her likes and dislikes were not always what you expected. For one thing, she didn't have much time for Dr. Johnson. She seemed to think he was more of a literary buffoon, maybe an eighteenth-century Alexander Woollcott, than anything else. I used to think the reason she sort of looked down on him was that they were so much alike—she and Dr. Johnson. Both of them would take the floor at the drop of a hat (maybe even drop it themselves) and hold forth on any topic under the sun, as long as they had an audience, and they were both always pretty sure of having one. And both of them could be dogmatic. But, in a way, it was like she was ashamed of both Dr. Johnson and herself—for liking to talk so much and for enjoying people and everything else as much as they did. Maybe, in a way, she didn't think they were "professional" enough.

But then it might have all had something to do with the eighteenth century. Mrs. Edney never did seem to feel at home in the eighteenth century, even if she did come from a farm out at Louisa. She was always talking about the eighteenth century being so interested in *form* until they just didn't care *what* they wrote about as long as it had *form*; and she thought, in that respect, that it was terribly inferior to the nineteenth century, when there were poets who really *burned*. *The Rape of the Lock* was all right, but she always seemed to be afraid of liking it—or anything else she really got a kick out of—too much.

But Shakespeare and the Romantic Poets were her high particulars. We spent weeks on *Macbeth,* until I thought you just couldn't get any more out of that play. But it seemed like *Macbeth* was about something she was interested in more than nearly anything else—how far a man could let his ambition lead him or whether he ought to be ambitious at all. I think maybe she saw herself in Macbeth; she was always, in a way, trying to get away from Louisa, even though she kept one foot there, so to say. Maybe she was afraid, if she didn't watch out, she could get hard, too.

I remember one time she came down on me with both feet when I said I couldn't really sympathize with Macbeth when he began to regret killing Duncan and everything. She said, "Well, don't you feel sorry for him, even though he is getting what he deserves?" But I said, "If he had done right in the first place, he wouldn't have gotten in that fix at all." And then she looked at me a long time, and I thought maybe she thought I was being smart-alecky and was going to mow me down with some of her sarcasm. But she didn't; she just spoke sort of kindly and said, "Well, you're not making much allowance for human nature." I was terribly moral then and didn't come to see what she was talking about until later.

Keats and Shelley were *her* poets; they wrote about things that took the top of your head off and set you on fire, she said. Shelley's "To a Skylark" was a great favorite of hers, and she used to read it like she wished she could be that skylark and take off and never come back any more: "Higher still and higher. . . . " When she read Wordsworth's "The Solitary Reaper" aloud, I could tell that the highland girl's song seemed very close to her. Maybe she thought the highland girl was singing about her own Louisa and her own Barlow County and saying to the world: "This is all I have, but it is poetry, too." Then I remember when I came and told her I had read Keats' *The Eve of St. Agnes* and tried to tell her that it represented everything I had ever wanted in poetry. But she sort of cut me off like she couldn't bear to hear me talk about it, it was so beautiful. She said, "Yes, I know. Isn't that a lovely thing?" But right away she pulled herself up and asked me what I was going to read for my next book report. But I never forgot. I had seen, all in a minute, that Mrs. Edney *loved* what she taught. Maybe that was why she didn't like the eighteenth century. They were always having reasons and facts and systems, but maybe they didn't *love* anything.

Mrs. Edney liked Coleridge a lot, too. Anything that was mysterious always excited her. She read detective stories until one and two o'clock in the morning, and she was always worrying about what "Kubla Khan" and "Christabel" would have been like if Coleridge had been able to finish them. One time she told me she had been laying off for years to write an essay called "The Person from Porlock," which was going to be about the man that came and interrupted Coleridge while he was writing "Kubla Khan." She wondered what sort of man he was and what he wanted and why his business was so important that it wouldn't keep. I think she sort of regarded him as the demon that keeps anybody—let alone, Coleridge or any writer—from doing what he sets out to do or thinks he ought to do. But then that was just like her to want to turn everything over in her mind and see it from all sides.

She was certainly always doing that in literature, seeing both sides until it was hard to make up your mind what was really right. Maybe that was why she liked Henry James, who she said was a novelist's novelist. I know I tried to read him because she said that, but it just didn't seem to me he was worth the effort. After a while, you sort of got tired of all the sides old Henry was always seeing; you just wanted him to come out flat-footed and *tell* something. I told her what I thought about him; and she said, "Well, let him rest until you are older. Then give him another try." But, to tell the truth, I think she was just a little bored by Henry James herself. I think it was another case of her thinking she out to be "literary." Because she did like *excitement* in a novel, and I don't think she ever found much in Henry James. She didn't think there was anything better than a good *story*, and she wasn't ashamed to say she liked *Gone With the Wind*. She was particularly fond of Roark Bradford's Negro stories from the Bible. It was like *there* was something that stood for Louisa and Barlow County and West Tennessee to a fare-you-well, and yet it was "literary" and she could afford to let herself go all the way for it. It was almost like something she had had a hand in herself, and I don't doubt she could have told Roark Bradford a few West Tennessee stories he hadn't heard before.

I used to wonder sometimes if Mrs. Edney ever felt like she was wasted on Woodville. I knew they said that when she got her Master's degree at Vanderbilt, Dr. Mims had offered her a place in the

English Department there; she was certainly good enough to teach in a college. And yet she never gave any sign of being dissatisfied; in fact, she went out of her way, it looked like, to do things she didn't really have to—like directing the senior play and being faculty adviser for the school paper and teaching the Fellowship Class in the Methodist Sunday School. And she had Mr. Edney, too. The more things she got mixed up in, the more energy she seemed to have. It was almost like, in Mrs. Edney's case, the person from Porlock had really made her work harder than ever. Maybe it was like saying, "My strength is made perfect in weakness."

We all knew Mrs. Edney wasn't well, and the last year I was in high school she kept getting thinner and thinner and looking worse and worse. She said it was her gall bladder and it really ought to come out, but Mr. Edney wouldn't even let her talk about it. She told somebody he simply wouldn't go with her to the hospital if she had an operation, but all her friends had said they would be glad to go and stay with her. Still, she wouldn't do anything about it; she just kept on hurting. Then about a month before school was out, she had to have an emergency operation. The doctors had said there was no doubt about it; she had cancer. When they operated, though, it was so far gone that they had to take out nearly all her stomach. But when she found out about it, she said she could eat it back into shape in no time. She even told me what the doctor said to her when she was recuperating: "You don't know how good you look to me because, sister, I've seen your insides."

Everybody felt like she couldn't last much longer, but nobody wanted to say it. So when fall came round and she insisted on going back to teaching, there wasn't anything to do but go on and let her. Just before I went off to college I went down to see her. I felt like it might be the last time I would ever see her, and I wanted somehow to tell her what she had meant to me. But I was afraid it would upset her; she was always afraid of loving things in front of other people. So I just said, "Mrs. Edney, you know I think I'm going to major in English." She looked at me with that old look that seemed to search you out from head to heel in a flat second, and I think she knew what I was trying to say because she said, "Well, I hope you won't forget *everything* I've tried to teach you."

She died two days after Thanksgiving. They said she never would admit how bad she was hurting and wouldn't even stay in the bed until right at the end; she couldn't bear to give up, I guess. She had fought so long against people who didn't like poetry and believed in "practical" education; there was no reason why she couldn't lick cancer. When I heard that she was dead, I could hardly believe it. You just couldn't associate death with all that energy and love. I remembered so much about her that it hurt to even think about her. And then I thought about something she had said once about Heaven—that maybe it was where you could work forever without anybody bothering you and do all the things you hadn't been able to do before. Finally, I remembered something she had told me one day when we were having an argument about the use of *shall* and *will*. She said, "You can use *will* in the first person when you are expressing determination. Why, don't you know, when you take the baptismal vows in the Methodist Church, you say, 'God being my help, I *will*'?" The more I thought about it, the more I thought maybe that was what *she* had always said—even when it came to the person from Porlock.

13

Uncle John

and the Trail of the Years

My Uncle John was a Methodist preacher; now that he was retired, he and Aunt Estelle lived in Woodville. He had kept a diary for over sixty years, and every week he wrote a piece for the *Barlow County Appeal* called "Down the Trail of the Years." It was usually about when he and Daddy and the other Drake boys were growing up out at Maple Grove and what all went on at the Maple Grove Methodist Church and in the Drake and other families out there. I used to think it was kind of monotonous, about all those folks that had been dead and gone for so long, but all the old people around town liked it.

Uncle John always said times certainly weren't like they used to be. There weren't any more men now like Uncle Reek Wood (his name was really Resin) and Uncle Razz Burks, whose name was really Erasmus, and Uncle Ralph Meadows, only the Drakes all pronounced it like it was spelled "Rafe." They were all fine upstanding men and not afraid of anything on earth, and their word was as good as their bond. They were always glad to see you when you went to their houses, and they didn't like anything better than just sitting around talking. It didn't matter what it was about; they just like to *talk*. Uncle Reek's wife was Grandma Drake's aunt, and Grandma always taught her family to think "Aunt" was the best cook in the world. Boiled hams and coconut cakes in five layers were her specialties; and sometimes, when it was a very special occasion, she would bring out the blackberry wine she had put up in the summer.

But Uncle John said things weren't like that any more. Nobody like to sit around and just talk these days. They were either too busy trying to make a million dollars, or else, when they did have time to sit down and relax, they wanted somebody up in New York or Chicago to be entertaining them over the radio or television. And then, of course, there just weren't any good cooks like Aunt any more because people just didn't care what they ate now as long as it wasn't any trouble to fix. They would just take it out of the deep-freeze or add hot water or do whatever it said on the box, and that was that—and usually tasted like it, too. And you never saw any country ham any more because people could make more money selling their hogs on the hoof. But nobody could have cooked it like Aunt anyway, Uncle John said. That used to make Mamma mad because she said she thought she could cook a country ham about as well as any white woman she ever saw; she would tell Daddy, "Thunderation! John just lives in the past, and neither one of you need to go on about those hams Aunt used to cook. Because if Aunt was alive today and could cook you one of those fool hams like she used to, it wouldn't taste the same because the truth is that you're positively getting *old*." And then she would straighten up and look around like now she had gotten *that* out of her system.

But Mamma or nobody else could do anything with Uncle John when he got his mind on the trail of the years or anything else he really wanted to do, like going down in the middle of July and cleaning off the Drakes' lot at Mt. Moriah Cemetery or going fish-ing all by himself down at Long Lake in the fall. Aunt Estelle was fifteen years younger than he was, and they had been married for nearly fifty years. But she said, "I just don't say anything to Mus-ter Drake (she always said 'Muster' instead of 'Mister' because she had taught elocution, Mamma said) any more about anything he wants to do. I figure that anybody that's over eighty years old and in as good health as he is after all these years can do whatever they want to."

And it was a good thing Aunt Estelle felt that way because Un-cle John usually did do what he wanted to. But she had had a lot of experience making the best of things. Uncle John had preached all over the Memphis Conference of the Methodist Church for thirty-five years--usually out on a circuit. And just about the time they got settled in one place, along would come the Conference and pick them up and move them somewhere else. So Aunt Estelle had been around a lot—even if it wasn't anywhere but in the Memphis Conference. She was always talking about Mrs. Somebody that she knew when they lived in So-and-so or something that happened when they lived somewhere else. I think Mamma got sort of tired always hearing about it, but I was kind of glad she had all those things to talk about because it looked like to me she ought to have something to show for all that thirty-five years of moving around and never having a house of her own.

Aunt Estelle taught elocution on the side, only now they called it "expression." We were always having to go to one of her recitals and hear children give "readings" about misbehaving in company or getting into hot water at school or something. Sometimes one of the older girls that was real thin and sad-eyed would give a musical reading that was all about somebody's lost lover or their broken troth, and my cousin Lina would play "To a Wild Rose" or Schubert's "Serenade" back behind the stage. And then everybody would dab at their eyes when it was over and say it was real sweet. Every now and then at the Thursday Study Club or the Euterpe Music Circle, Aunt Estelle would give a reading herself—like the one everybody liked about the little girl riding on the back seat and trying to tell her father how to drive. When she got to the part where a motorcycle policeman was chasing them, she would say, real innocently, "Daddy, that policeman looks like he wants to speak to you. Daddy, does he know you?" Aunt Estelle had snow-white hair and weighed nearly two hundred pounds, so everybody always laughed right there.

But I always thought maybe Aunt Estelle was sort of inclined to elocute even when she wasn't giving a reading, because she did seem to enjoy getting up in the air over things. I remember one time when I went to Memphis with her and Uncle John to have their feet worked on at the chiropodist's. We left home before day because they had to get back to Woodville for a funeral, and it was so dark you couldn't see your hand before your face, and raining hard, too. There had been a lot of high water that year, but it was supposed not to have gotten over the road or anything. We were riding along, and Uncle John and Aunt Estelle were having an argument about who Aunt Ellen Wood's mother-in-law had been

before she married when all of a sudden Aunt Estelle looked out
the window and hollered, "Oh, Daddy, you're right here on the
Loosahatchie Levee, and there's water all around. Slow down
quick! If we ran off the levee, we'd all be drowned!" It like to have
scared me to death, but Uncle John didn't even look to the right or
left. He just drove right on like he had heard it all a million times
before. Finally, I got up nerve enough to look out the window and
see all the water that we would run into if anything happened, and
I couldn't see anything but an old Poland China sow rooting around
in a field of last year's corn. We didn't come to the levee for another half hour.

One thing Uncle John was death on was taking pictures. He
must have had a camera since before Christ, Mamma said; all down
the years he had been taking pictures of everybody in the Drake
family at all ages and on all occasions. He also made pictures for
the public—weddings and graduations and things like that. But
every now and then he got into some kind of strange things in the
picture business.

Back during the war he had quite a run on taking pictures of
dead people all laid out in their coffins so their loved ones in service overseas could see how they looked before they were put
away. It looked like Uncle John didn't care what he was making a
picture *of*; he just wanted to get it down for the *record*, like he said.
And every Christmas, sure as shooting, we had to have a "group"
picture taken at one of the family dinners (we always had five—
one at each of the Drake brothers' houses). Mamma said she didn't
see any use in all that since every year everybody was just getting
older and uglier—and the Drakes never had been noted, you might
say, for their beauty in the first place. But Uncle John would just
shake his head and say, well, in years to come we would be awful
glad to have them because of the dear ones that had gone on, and
then he would start talking about Grandma and Pa, and all the
Drakes would start tuning up, and that was that. They were all like
that about the family and the old days.

Uncle John saved old letters and old newspaper clippings and
everything else, it looked like, that was old. He said he reckoned
he wouldn't ever have any use for them but he just liked to have
records of everything. He even kept old funeral notices and clippings of the columns he used to write for the *Barlow County Appeal*

when he was a young man out at Maple Grove that he signed "Snowflake." And he had so many scrapbooks stacked up in his library that he could hardly find any place for the new books he was always getting, like *Peloubet's Select Notes*, that was a Sunday-by-Sunday commentary on the International Sunday School lesson, and the *Christian Advocate* and all the other church magazines he took. I used to think it was kind of silly for Uncle John to save everything just because it was old, things that it looked like he never would have any *use* for. And I guess I never did really understand until that Christmas he and Aunt Estelle got their new car.

Uncle John and Aunt Estelle's only son, Stuart, had been killed in the war, and Uncle John had been crazy about him. He was tall and blond and handsome, and I was always wild about him because, even though he was ten years older than I was, he would tell me all about the courses he was taking in college and ask me what I wanted to study when I went off to school; and I wanted to be just like him when I grew up: warm and loving and true. We all thought Uncle John had taken Stuart's death pretty well, for all that Stuart had really been the apple of his eye. But Uncle John didn't talk about Stuart much any more and never even mentioned his name in "Down the Trail of the Years," and I thought maybe it was true what people said about Time being the Great Healer.

Now Uncle John and Aunt Estelle had only a daughter, Mary Virginia, who lived over in Greenville and was married to Albert Sidney Johnston Hurt that had done awfully well in the Ford business over there. Mary Virginia and Albert Sidney were always doing things for Aunt Estelle and Uncle John, and I used to wonder why they didn't try to get them a better car. The car they had had belonged to Stuart, and he had bought it secondhand when he was in college. It was nearly fifteen years old, but Uncle John kept it in perfect condition (Daddy said it ran like a sewing machine). And you could see him and Aunt Estelle riding out to Maple Grove or out to Fisher's Crossing, where she had grown up, most any time you wanted to. Uncle John would be looking straight ahead and driving as fast as the car would go, and Aunt Estelle would be holding on to the door handle and hollering at him over all the noise to slow down.

Finally, one Christmas Eve, Albert Sidney called Uncle John and told him to bring the car over to Greenville; he wanted to put some new seat covers on it. And when he and Aunt Estelle got over there, Albert Sidney had a brand-new Ford all ready and waiting for them as a Christmas present. But you know, the funniest thing was that they had a hard time at first making Uncle John give up the old car. He said he wanted to keep it just because it had been Stuart's. Stuart had been dead nearly ten years, but Uncle John said he just wished he could keep the old car, even if it didn't do anything but just sit out there in the yard where he could look out the window and see it every now and then. He said he was an old man and that was all that he had left now of his darling boy.

14

Brother Haynes

and the Nine-Year-Old

Evangelist

Everybody in town had seen the signs telling about the nine-year-old evangelist that was going to hold a meeting down at the Pentecostal Holiness Church. Her name was Ruby Nell Burns, and she was from Memphis. I never had been to a meeting at the Holiness Church before, but I sort of looked down on them because most of the people who went to church there had just moved into town from out in the country. But Daddy used to admire them because he said they weren't like the Methodists; they hadn't forgotten that people needed to be saved and hadn't sold their birthright to a lot of Yankees like the Southern Methodists had when they got amalgamated with the Northern Methodists in 1939.

The Holiness people had just moved into a new church out on the highway that Daddy said the Lord only knew where they got the money to build, and it was still unfinished. The brick veneer hadn't yet been put on, and all you could see was just concrete blocks. And they had a blue neon cross over the front door. Their preacher was a man named Brother Otis Haynes, that Daddy said was a good man, even if he did carry a comb instead of a pocketknife. (Daddy said no man could preach the Gospel without a pocketknife, so he gave Brother Haynes one out of the store.)

Brother Haynes' wife always looked like she had been ironing all day long but hadn't gotten around to the dress she had on, and they had a boy named Melvin and a girl named Merlene. Mamma used to make out like she was tired of hearing Daddy talk so much about Brother Haynes. She would say, "Oh, Jucks (which was Daddy's nickname that nobody knew why he was called by), you make me tired talking about that old Holy Roller preacher like he was a saint. He's just a *man,* and you remember what Aunt Bessie Moss' sister used to say. She said she'd never seen a man yet you could trust below the waistband of his pants." Daddy didn't like for her to talk that way, though, because, after all, Brother Haynes *was* a preacher.

Anyhow, it was my first summer at home after I had gone off to college, and I thought I would just like to go down and see a nine-year-old evangelist in operation. So I asked Jane Ferguson and Mary Katherine Wilkes, who had just started to high school, if they would like to go too. I didn't want to go by myself, and I couldn't find anybody my own age that wanted to go. Just before we left Jane's house, her grandmother, old Mrs. Ferguson, who was a pillar of the Methodist missionary society, said, "Now, Jane, don't you all go down there and laugh and try to make fun of those people. Just remember that they may be getting something down there they couldn't get at our church. They probably wouldn't feel at home anywhere else." Jane said, "No'm, we won't," and we got in the car and drove off.

It was a hot night, like when all your clothes stick to you and everybody says, "I declare, it's so close you can hardly breathe." There was a big crowd inside the church already, and all those people sitting there didn't make it any cooler. The permanent lighting fixtures hadn't been installed (I guess they didn't have enough money yet), and there weren't any screens on the windows. There were hundreds of candle-flies swarming around the dazzling bare light globes that were hanging from the ceiling, and everybody was fanning as hard as he could. There were a lot of women with babies, and sometimes they would just haul off and nurse them right there in front of everybody, which I thought was sort of uncalled-for.

I looked around to see if I saw anybody I knew, but the only people I recognized were some people from out at Haley's Switch that I saw every Saturday in the store. But there was lots going on all around the church. People got up to talk to their friends; a lot of women seemed to be catching up on their visiting, even if they had all probably seen each other there the night before. Because the Holiness Church was practically always having a revival. They didn't ever seem like they got religion enough to last them out a spell without being continually revived. They were supposed to be terrible big believers in backsliding, though, so I guessed they knew what they were doing.

After a while Mrs. Haynes came in and sat down at the piano and started playing "Sweet Hour of Prayer." It was an old upright that looked like it had been hauled all over the county in the back of a pick-up truck, and sounded a good deal like it too. Then Brother Haynes came in and announced the first hymn. It was "Blessed Assurance." Everybody sang it through and then went right on into "Rescue the Perishing." I knew that the Holiness people shouted, and I wanted to hear them. I never had heard anybody shout before—certainly not at the Methodist Church. (Daddy said Methodists had gotten too respectable to shout, and he thought it was their loss.) But when it started, it was pretty much like I expected. After a while different people began to holler out "Hallelujah!" and "Amen" and things like that. That didn't stop the singing, though; and they would just go right on from one hymn into another without even a breathing-spell. It looked like they could go on all night—Mrs. Haynes at the piano and the people out in the congregation.

I looked at Mary Katherine and Jane to see how they were holding up, and they looked like they didn't know exactly *how* to act. They acted like they wanted to smile but then seemed to change their minds about it, not because they were afraid but because they didn't exactly understand what was going on. I felt like all this singing was leading up to something like a climax, and I began to get that prickly feeling all over like you do at a wedding when the bride's mother has just come in and you know that the "Wedding March" is bound to be next. All of a sudden, I heard a commotion in the vestibule at the back of the auditorium, and then I saw a little girl with long golden curls and a snow-white cloak on coming down the aisle with a white Bible under her arm. Behind her there was a tall, stout woman, between fifty and sixty, the kind that I used to be afraid of when they played policewomen or cruel stepmothers in the movies, with a blue polka-dot dress and a blue bolero on and a blue felt hat that looked like a Scotch tam. She followed the little girl all the way down the aisle, but, when the little girl stepped up onto the platform, she sat down in one of the front pews. And she looked like she was right glad to sit down. I think her corset was probably laced up too tight, and she sat there straight as a poker with her lips folded tight and didn't say a word to anybody.

When the little girl got up on the platform, she knelt down to one side of the pulpit with her back to the congregation and prayed. When she got through, she took off her cloak; and she had on a white organdy dress tied with a pink satin sash, like little girls wore to birthday parties, along with a bow-ribbon just like it in their hair.

When they got through with the hymn they were singing, Brother Haynes stepped up to the pulpit and said, "Friends, this is the little girl that has come to bring us the Gospel message this week. She has come all the way from Memphis, which is so full of sinners that it positively stinks with the smell of corruption. It's a wonder anybody can stay pure in that infernal place; it's like a modern Sodom or Gomorrah. But, thank God, Ruby Nell has been preserved unspotted and has been sent by the Lord to save souls in this sinful community. Ruby Nell, we're proud that you can be with us tonight."

And then she stood up, and you could hardly see her over the pulpit. All you could see was just a small round face with long curls floating down behind. But then she stood up on something behind the pulpit—probably a Coca-Cola case turned upside down—and you could see her better. I wondered what she would sound like when she talked, and, as soon as she spoke, I knew that she sounded just like I had figured she would. She had a sort of nasal voice but not too whiny, and it seemed to fall at the end of every sentence. But it was her eyes you noticed most. They were dark brown, and they really seemed to burn. And I thought about the coal of fire that one of the seraphim had laid on Isaiah's lips.

Her sermon was mainly about when she got her call to the ministry. Ruby Nell was an orphan, and she was being brought up by the lady sitting in the front row (everybody called her Sister Burns). One Sunday while she was listening to the sermon in church, Ruby Nell had a vision of Jesus standing on a hill with a flock of sheep down below in a valley. He was trying to say something to her, but she couldn't make it out. But, all of a sudden, she realized He must be telling her to go preach the Gospel. And so, at the age of five, she started preaching around in the neighborhood and at Sunday School until finally Sister Burns decided that Ruby Nell really was called to the Lord's work and started taking her around to churches all over the country.

Somewhere along the line Ruby Nell held up a picture she had painted of her vision, but we were sitting so far back that it didn't look like much in particular but a lot of bright blobs of paint on a black background. I never did see Jesus. But everybody seemed to be terribly moved. Every now and then somebody would holler out something like "Oh, Lord, ain't she a darling little angel?" By the time she stopped preaching, a lot of people were crying, men and women both. But it wasn't time yet to call the sinners up to the mourners' bench, because Brother Haynes hadn't had a chance to pray yet and they hadn't taken up the collection.

So Brother Haynes started off praying, and I thought maybe now I would get to hear them talk in the Unknown Tongue, like they were supposed to do when the Spirit moved them. So when he started praying, I kept my eyes open so I could see how he looked when the Spirit got hold of him. Every now and then Brother Haynes would clench both his fists right in the middle of a sentence and shout "Hallelujah! Hallelujah!" with his eyes still shut. And then he would drop his voice down so low that you could hardly hear him. Every now and then somebody in the congregation would shout, but I kept looking at Brother Haynes. Every time he clenched his fists and shouted, I felt like he was trying to catch hold of something and couldn't. And I wondered if he still had that pocketknife Daddy had given him.

Nobody—Brother Haynes or anybody else—talked in the Unknown Tongue that night. I guess he wanted everybody to know exactly what he was praying for because he kept strictly to English. He prayed for the United States and all our allies and for all the missionaries in the home field and in the foreign field and for all the sick that God had visited with His afflicting hand and for all the sinners everywhere that weren't saved and especially for those in West Tennessee.

When it looked like he had run out of things to pray about, he quit; it was time to take up the collection. Brother Haynes said how proud they all were to have such a darling little saint in their midst—and Sister Burns too—and that now they would take up a collection to pay Ruby Nell's expenses. Then he asked Sister Burns to say a few words, and she rose up down in the front. She didn't seem to be the least bit nervous about speaking. She just looked like everything about her—her corset, her tight lips, and all—seemed to be pulling her back in, like a bit in a horse's mouth. She turned around to face the congregation but kept one hand on the back of the pew, like she might be trying to brace herself or something. Then she said, "Friends, Ruby Nell and I are proud to be doing the Lord's work in your midst, but you all know that the laborer is worthy of his hire. So I want to assure you that not a penny that you give us tonight will be wasted. Ruby Nell is a sweet little angel, and I hope and pray she may be spared for many years to continue her ministry to the hardened sinners in West Tennessee." Then she sat down, and I thought I saw her dab at her eyes with her handkerchief.

As soon as they got through taking up the collection, Brother Haynes and Ruby Nell began to call mourners to come up and get reconciled. But they didn't have to work very hard at it because Ruby Nell had already worked them up to a pretty high pitch. People would just go up and fling themselves down on the railing at the foot of the platform, and Brother Haynes and Ruby Nell would come along and talk to them real quietly. But, sometimes, Ruby Nell would call out, "God bless you, brother, for saying those words," and then she would move on down the line to the next one.

We didn't stay very long after that, even if the meeting *was* going to go on till midnight. But when we got outside, we didn't talk very much. Except Jane said, "I wonder what grade that little girl is in at school, or do they make her go to school like everybody else?" And Mary Katherine said, "I wonder if she ever wore that dress to a party or anything." Then we all went and had an icecream cone before we went home.

The next morning I told Mamma and Daddy all about Ruby Nell and Brother Haynes and everything. Mamma acted like she just wasn't going to *let* herself say anything, but Daddy must have thought I was trying to make fun of them because he got off all over

again on having too much education and getting above your raising and acting a fool. A few days later he told us that Uncle John,
the Methodist preacher, had been down to hear Ruby Nell and
thought she was right smart. But he didn't look at Mamma when
he was telling us about it. Mamma just sort of pulled in the corners
of her mouth and *looked* at me, but she didn't say a word.

Several weeks later Daddy came home to dinner one day and
looked like he was mad about something, only he didn't want to
tell us what it was. After a while Mamma decided he had pouted
long enough, so she said, "Jucks, what *is* the matter? Is something
wrong down at the store?"

He said, "Naw! It's just that fool Preacher Haynes. You know
what he did? He ran off over to Hot Springs, Arkansas, with a
woman from over in Monroe County; and they had to send over
there and bring him back home." I wanted to laugh, but I looked
at Daddy and decided I'd better not. Mamma didn't say a word,
and we finally got through dinner—somehow.

We didn't talk much about Brother Haynes after that. He and
his family soon moved away, down in Mississippi, and I never did
find out who the woman he ran off with was. The Pentecostal Holiness Church got a new preacher, and, after a while, people quit
talking about Brother Haynes. But Mamma never seemed to forget
him. For a long time afterward, whenever Daddy would start telling her how uncharitable she was for saying that somebody was
mean or dishonest or something, she would straighten up and look
at me right quick and say, "All right, Robert, you remember about
Brother Haynes, don't you?" Daddy never would say anything
after that.

15

Mr. Andrew

and the Big Cedar Tree

I had heard about Mr. Andrew Fowler all my life. He was kind of kin to Aunt Estelle, so we never could say much about him in the family—or at least in front of her. But there were enough other people talking about him to make up for that. Used to, they wouldn't talk about him in front of me; then, after I got in high school, they must have decided I knew about things and they might as well.

Mr. Andrew's folks were one of the oldest families in the county, but Daddy said every family had to have a black sheep and Mr. Andrew must be it for the Fowlers. He had married Miss Lucy Brinkley from over in Monroe County, and they had two children that were grown and married. And then one day, when he was about fifty, Mr. Andrew just proceeded to leave home and go off and live with another woman. She was one of the Hughes girls named Florene, and she had hoed a right wide row in her day, Daddy said. I never did think she was pretty or even very good looking, for that matter, but I just guessed it was because Mr. Andrew was getting old. (Daddy said, as much as Mr. Andrew had stepped around, he was surprised he could still cut the mustard.)

The worst part of it was that Mr. Andrew and Florene went to live out on the edge of town, right down in the middle of some Negro houses that Mr. Andrew owned. There they were, right where everybody could pass by any time of day and see them. (I think that was why lots of people objected to Mr. Andrew—he was such an open scandal, with all that going on right there in your face.) Florene's old father and mother lived right down the road a piece from them, and everybody thought it was too bad for them that Florene was going on that way in their old age. And I used to wonder why Mr. and Mrs. Hughes didn't just rise up and lay Mr. Andrew and Florene out for the way they were going on, but Daddy said Mr. Andrew owned the house the Hugheses were living in and they were too old to do much of anything about it.

Mr. Andrew's wife, Miss Lucy, still lived on in the big old house just off the square; a lot of people wondered why she didn't go on and divorce Mr. Andrew. She certainly had grounds enough, and she had some money of her own so she wasn't entirely dependent on him. But she wouldn't do a thing about it. I know because one time Aunt Estelle, who was really kin to Mr. Andrew and not to her, simply asked her about it. (Of course, Mamma always said that Aunt Estelle had enough brass to ask anybody anything—kin to them or not.) And Miss Lucy said, "No, I'm not going to divorce him. Because he's a lot older than she is, and, when he gets old, she'll leave him for a younger man. And somebody'll have to take care of him then." But Aunt Estelle said she just thought Miss Lucy was plain silly. She said *she'd* never do a thing like that, but, then, of course, Uncle John wasn't about to step out on her either.

But Mr. Andrew and Florene just went right on and didn't seem to bother what people were saying about them. And it looked like they were happy because Mr. Andrew bought her a Ford car and a big diamond ring, but then, of course, they didn't ever go anywhere but just stayed right down there with all the Negroes. And naturally nobody ever went to see them. Mr. Andrew had a lot of farm land, and he stayed busy attending to all that, so there wasn't much for Florene to do but just sit around out there and manicure her nails and go down and see her mother and father a couple of times a day.

Of course, when she came into town once a week to get her hair set at the beauty parlor, everybody would notice her, and some of the high school boys would even whistle at her. But she just went right on down the street without looking to the left or right, like she knew exactly what she was doing and didn't need any help in the process. I never did see her, though, without thinking her eyes looked just like the fox's in Mamma's fur neckpiece. They were just as black and shiny and cold looking, and I remember thinking that I sure would hate to be standing between her and anything she really wanted.

Well, the years went along, and I went off to college. But every time I came home somebody would be sure to say something about Mr. Andrew and Florene. Nobody was much shocked about them any more, but they kept on talking about them anyhow because they were always right there and you could always prove anything by pointing to them. In a way, it was like they sort of belonged to everybody in town.

Mr. Andrew kept getting older and even a little feeble, and people began to wonder how long it would be before Florene left him for somebody younger and with maybe more money. But nothing happened until one day Jack Ellis came breezing into town in a brand-new red Buick to sell Negro insurance, and he and Florene took one look at each other and that was that. He was short and fat and used lots of Vitalis on his hair, but Florene must have really fallen for him. I don't know what he saw in her because she was at least ten years older than he was and beginning to dye her hair, but I reckon he thought she was going to come into a lot of money when Mr. Andrew died if he could just hold on until then.

Nobody knew what kind of story Florene told Mr. Andrew, but her father was an invalid now and maybe she told him she had to go down and sit up with her father at night while her mother got some rest from nursing him in the daytime. Anyhow, Mr. Andrew was old himself now and didn't go out very much, and lots of times you could drive along the road about suppertime and see him sitting out on his front porch looking down the road toward the house where Mr. and Mrs. Hughes lived. There was a big old cedar tree in Mr. Andrew's front yard, and sometimes he would just be sitting there watching the sun go down behind the cedar tree.

Finally, that spring after Jack Ellis had come to town back in the winter, Mr. Andrew got sick in the bed; and somebody said he really had a bad heart, and it was just a matter of time. And everybody knew that as soon as he died and Florene got her hands on the money he was supposed to leave her, she and Jack Ellis would get married. And it was kind of funny because, strangely enough, people sort of felt sorry for Mr. Andrew for the way Florene was doing him. There he was out there all by himself, all old and sick and separated from his family, and Florene was running around in that red Buick with Jack Ellis.

Nobody ever did know how Mr. Andrew found out what was going on. I don't know who would have been brave enough to tell him. He didn't really have any friends except his tenants—black and white—and they certainly wouldn't have wanted to get mixed up in something like that. And, anyhow, maybe nobody really told him anything, but he guessed it. Anyhow, it was summer time, and Florene began to go down more and more to sit up with her father. And a couple of times she stayed all night. But she would always take Mr. Andrew his breakfast when she went back in the morning.

Fourth of July morning, Charlie Titus, one of Mr. Andrew's colored tenants that lived next door, saw Florene going in about seven-thirty with Mr. Andrew's breakfast tray, and then, after a while, he heard what sounded like a couple of explosions. But he didn't pay much mind to it because all the children around were beginning to shoot their holiday firecrackers. Then about ten o'-clock, Charlie Titus went over to Mr. Andrew's like he always did to see if Mr. Andrew had anything for him to do around the yard or in the house. Charlie Titus couldn't make anybody hear at the back door, and he hadn't seen anybody leave, so he finally just went right on in. There wasn't a sign of anybody around, so he just proceeded on in to Mr. Andrew's bedroom to see if he was sicker than usual or something. And there was Florene stretched out across the bed where she had fallen and Mr. Andrew lying back in his night shirt with a double-barrelled shotgun still in his hands—both of them dead.

And then people really did turn loose and talk. Of course a lot of them said how sorry they felt for Miss Lucy and Andrew, Jr., and Katherine, but it just went to show about the wages of sin and all. But what really stood people on end was when they read Mr. Andrew's will that very afternoon and everybody found out that he hadn't given Florene a thing but had left everything to Miss Lucy and the children. And in the will he said he didn't want them to have any kind of funeral service for him, but just to bury him out under the big cedar tree in his front yard.

All kinds of tales went around then, sure enough. Somebody even told it that Harry Pipkin, the jeweler, sent word up to the funeral home that they better not bury Florene with that ring on because Mr. Andrew hadn't finished paying for it. But what really scandalized folks was when they really did bury Mr. Andrew out under the cedar tree—but not before they had had a big funeral at the Methodist Church. (Andrew, Jr., was on the Board of Stewards.) The Hugheses all buried their folks out at Poplar Springs, so that's where they took Florene—both funerals at three o'clock the next afternoon because nobody wanted to go to both, I guess, not even in Woodville. I don't know what became of Jack Ellis, but he and that red Buick were sort of scarce around town for the next few days.

Finally, everything around town seemed to settle down, and everybody got to talking about something else besides Mr. Andrew and Florene. But then a week after they had buried Mr. Andrew under the big cedar tree, they took him up and buried him in the Fowlers' lot at Oakwood Cemetery, and that started everybody going again. They said Miss Lucy wanted to leave him where he was, but Andrew, Jr., and Katherine insisted that they move him and said it would be all right now—since they had officially fulfilled the terms of the will. A lot of people, especially the Methodists, said Andrew, Jr., and Katherine had done the right thing. They said that Mr. Andrew had shamed his family enough while he was alive without adding to it after he was dead. But every time I thought about it, I remembered how Mr. Andrew used to sit there on the porch all by himself watching the sun go down behind the big cedar tree, and I couldn't help wishing they had left him right there where he had wanted to be.

16

Daddy

and the Bull

Named Herbert

Herbert Fisher was Aunt Estelle Drake's brother, so he really wasn't any kin to us. But we saw a lot of him and his wife, Sara Kate, because they were always going out to Uncle John and Aunt Estelle's. Aunt Estelle always called him "Brother," but the rest of the Drakes called him "Herbert."

Herbert used to make Daddy so mad he could nearly die because he was so lazy and he hadn't ever done anything he didn't want to do. His father owned a store and a lot of farm land out at Fisher's Crossing, and Herbert hadn't ever done anything much but sit around the store and every now and then sell a nickel box of snuff to one of the Negroes. Daddy said he had always been lying around on flowery beds of ease and that it all came of being born with a silver spoon in your mouth. Herbert was the biggest talker you ever heard, though; and he wouldn't stop for anybody, even Daddy. I used to tell Daddy that was why Herbert made him mad; but Daddy would just snort and say, "It just makes me mad to look at him. He hasn't ever done a decent day's work in his life; and everything he has, somebody has given him. First, his father, and then Miss Pearl." Miss Pearl was Herbert and Aunt Estelle's sister; and she was married to Mr. Jim Rucker, who had made a lot of money in the furniture business down in Alabama. She was always doing things for Herbert and Aunt Estelle, too.

But Herbert was so particular that he was hard to do anything for. When Miss Pearl wanted to give him a television set, she gave him the money and told him to go ahead and buy one, but Herbert traveled all over West Tennessee looking at different kinds and trying to figure out which would be the best buy. He like to have run everybody crazy talking about why one brand was better than another and what was really wrong with this kind and that one. Finally, Miss Pearl just took the money away from him and went and bought one for him herself and had it sent out to his house and installed. And she had to do the same way when she wanted to give him an air conditioner; she just bought it and had it put in before Herbert could say pea-turkey.

Aunt Estelle used to tell me a lot about him because she thought he was awfully funny, even if he was her brother. She said, "Brother is the scariest man in the world. And he's always afraid that he's going to catch something or other. One time when I had had a bad cold and was just getting over it, I thought I would take him out a book I had been reading since he was sick in bed with lumbago. But when I got there, he said he didn't want to read the book. Sara Kate was kind of puzzled and tried to make him go on and take it, but I said, 'Now, Sara Kate, I've known Brother longer than you have. And I know as well as anything that he is simply afraid he'll get some of my cold germs from reading that book.'"

But the funniest tale Aunt Estelle ever told about Herbert was about the time when he and Sara Kate were married. She said, "Brother has always been the biggest old maid in the world about his clothes. The night before he got married, do you know what he made me do? Well, he had bought himself some new silk pajamas to wear on his honeymoon. But he was afraid they didn't fit him exactly right. So the night before the wedding, he put them on and walked up and down the front stairs out at home and made me stand there at the foot of the stairs and watch him to see if they were hanging right in the seat." It used to make Daddy perfectly furious to hear about it because the idea of a *man* sleeping in silk pajamas was so absurd to him. He slept in an old-fashioned nightgown himself.

But nothing Herbert did in the clothes line surprised Daddy, after a while. He said, "Herbert's the beatenest thing I ever saw.

Why, when he goes over to Mary Virginia's in Greenville—his own niece—to spend the day on Sunday, he takes along another suit in a suitcase just to wear to church. And every time he sits down, he creases his pants just to make sure he won't lose the crease that's in there."

And even Uncle John used to make fun of Herbert. Of course, Uncle John couldn't say too much because Herbert was Aunt Estelle's brother, and, after all, Uncle John *was* a Methodist preacher. But you could tell how he was feeling about things, just the same. One time Sara Kate's oldest brother, Mr. Jack Richardson, a big cattle man out in Texas, gave Herbert and Sara Kate a new car, and Uncle John said he just hated to see it because from then on Herbert was going to worry everybody to death taking care of that car. Uncle John said, "Every time he goes out to get in the car, he'll look to see if there's a scratch on it anywhere or look to see if maybe one fender isn't higher than the other."

And Uncle John wasn't above teasing Herbert out in public. One time Herbert and Sara Kate were spending the weekend out at Uncle John's house, and Herbert went to Sunday School with him. Herbert had taught the Men's Bible Class out at Fisher's Crossing off and on for years, and he had never been to Sunday School anywhere else. So when he and Uncle John got home from church and a lot of the family were all around, Uncle John said, in a loud voice, "Herbert, when you got up there at the church this morning and saw all those folks sitting there that you didn't know, weren't you just a little *scared*?" And then Uncle John just died laughing, but it didn't bother Herbert a bit. Things like that never did get under his skin. You could tease him to a fare-you-well, and it wouldn't faze him at all. Mamma said, "I think Herbert just enjoys being peculiar and kind of prides himself on it." And it looked like it was so because you couldn't ever make him mad, and Daddy certainly tried hard enough. But Herbert would just shake his head and slap his knee and laugh and go right on talking until you just wanted to scream, or at least that's the way Mamma said it made her feel.

Herbert was always complaining about something. He always thought the hands on his place were stealing from him, and he was always trying to catch up with them. He was always coming in Drake Brothers' store and telling Daddy and Uncle Buford what he suspected somebody out there of doing. And finally Uncle Buford, who never spoke up until he had something right strong to say, said, "Well, Herbert, I don't see why you're complaining so much about that fellow. He's making a living for you and him both." And Daddy got so tickled he nearly died because he said it certainly was the truth. Daddy said, "Herbert has always had everything just dumped right in his lap. Even the hands on his place were born there. He's got one nigger out there named Johnnie B. that is the third generation of niggers to live on that place, and there're more of them coming along all the time. And Herbert doesn't really have to do anything on the place at all; the niggers do all the work. I told him the other day that he was the best window farmer I ever saw. He just sits there at the window all day long and looks out in the field and tries to see what the niggers are doing, but he doesn't lift a finger himself. Why, he'd have been making a sharecrop now if it hadn't been for Miss Pearl and Sara Kate's brother."

The years went along, and Herbert got high blood pressure. And then he like to have run everybody crazy sure enough. Sara Kate wasn't well either. She was always having some kind of female trouble, and she had had just about all her organs taken out except her gizzard, Mamma said. Sara Kate was always nervous and was always telling you how bad she felt. And now Herbert was always telling you how bad *he* felt. Mamma said, "Herbert Fisher starts telling you how he feels before you've even had a chance to ask him. He's always patting his stomach and saying, 'Well, I'm getting fat, but I'm not going to get too fat. I'm doing just what the doctor tells me.' You can't make him hush, and he goes on until he's told you every single one of his symptoms." But nothing kept Herbert and Sara Kate from worrying about their health. They were always going to the doctor or having him come out to see them at Fisher's Crossing, and every now and then one of them would go out to the hospital for a couple of days for a check-up.

I think Uncle John got right tired of hearing all about it because one day when I was out at his house, he said, "Miss Estelle is going to read a paper tomorrow at the missionary meeting about imaginary illnesses, and I'll tell you there are some members of the family I would like to have read it and then reread it and commit it to memory. It looks like I haven't heard anything for the last forty years but about how they were feeling and all; to tell you the truth,

I'm just *tired* of it." I thought Mamma would get a kick out of that; but when I told her what he said, she sort of pursed her lips and said, "John has never been really sick himself, and he doesn't have any sympathy with anybody who is sick." But it seemed to me that maybe he had something there.

But what really made Mamma mad was when Cousin Edgar Powell said what he did. Cousin Edgar was one of Daddy's cousins that never did amount to much. He farmed a little piece of land that belonged to his wife, but mostly he was hanging around Drake Brothers waiting for somebody to buy him a Coke or give him a ride home. Daddy was always letting him have things on credit he knew he never would pay for, and I guess he appreciated it because he told Mamma one day that Daddy and Herbert Fisher were the best men he ever saw. It made Mamma so mad she liked to have died for him to put Daddy in the same class with Herbert. She said the only reason Herbert hadn't ever done anything wrong was that he didn't have sense enough to, and maybe hadn't had much of a chance to, either.

Herbert had had some close shaves, though. One time when he was running the store out at Fisher's Crossing, some Negro men came in and held everybody up. Sara Kate was up there at the time, and she was beside herself because she thought they were going to get her diamond rings, but they didn't. They just made Herbert open the safe and hand over all the cash he had on hand. It like to have scared him to death, and every time you started talking about anything happening to anybody, he would tell you about the time the store was held up. It used to provoke Mamma to hear about it so much, but Daddy enjoyed it because he said he just liked to think about somebody pulling a gun on Herbert and making him step around right lively. Daddy said, "I'll bet that's one time he didn't look to see if the creases in his pants were straight or not."

But then after Herbert got sick, he and Sara Kate didn't do much of anything. They had sold the store several years before, and now they just sat out there at Fisher's Crossing and thought about whether they were feeling as good today as they did yesterday or whether they might not feel worse tomorrow. Sara Kate didn't feel like doing much cooking, so they were always riding into town to eat at the Bluebird Cafe or somewhere else. Then they would go out to the hospital if there was anybody sick out there that they knew, or they would go up to the funeral home if anybody they knew was dead. And then when they didn't know where else to go, they would pile in out at Aunt Estelle's.

You could see them riding all over the county any time of day. Daddy seemed to think Herbert was trying to get Sara Kate's mind off her nerves, but Mamma said he was just restless and didn't know what else to do. He certainly wasn't doing anything out at Fisher's Crossing. Sara Kate had never liked the country, and she wanted to move back to town, where she had grown up. But Herbert was afraid the hands would steal everything on the place if he moved away. Daddy said, "Herbert might as well move to town for all the good he does out there. Why, there're parts of his farm he hasn't been over in five years. But he's so afraid something's going to go on out there that he doesn't know about. He's the kind that's just *looking* for something wrong. Just don't let me get started on him, it's so ridiculous to me." But Mamma said nobody had ever been able to stop Daddy or start him either if he didn't want to.

But then after Herbert got sick and all, it seemed like Mamma and Daddy were going out to see them all the time. I used to ask Mamma about it, and she would say, "I certainly get tired of going out there, but your Daddy gets restless sitting at home at night, and he likes to tease Herbert. So we go out there and listen to Herbert complain, and then about ten o'clock Sara Kate fixes us some instant Sanka. I hate to think that I will come to the time when I have to drink instant Sanka, but it looks like I'm there right now. But Herbert and Sara Kate are afraid that real coffee will keep them awake."

Well, anybody that knew Daddy very well would know he wasn't going to put up with Herbert forever without doing *something*. For one thing, Herbert was always bragging about his prize bull that Sara Kate's brother had sent them from Texas; it was Sara Kate's birthday, and the bull was a birthday present from Mr. Richardson. The express charges came to over a hundred dollars, and Herbert said if Mr. Richardson hadn't prepaid the charges, he would just have had to send that bull right on back to Texas. Well, anyway, Daddy got tired of always hearing Herbert tell about his prize bull. So when he and Uncle Buford got a new bull out at their farm, Daddy said they would just name him Herbert; maybe that would take care of Herbert Fisher for a while. So they named the bull Herbert; and everybody in the family thought it was a good joke, only nobody told Herbert about it. But the funniest thing was that, as time went on, it looked like they had made a poor investment. Mamma got a big kick out of it, though. When she was telling me about it, she said, "I always thought there was something wrong with that bull. He was the meekest, mildest-looking thing you ever saw. And I told your Daddy that if they named him Herbert, there was no telling what might happen. And it was the truth because that bull turned out to be just plain impotent." Then she just like to have killed herself laughing, but Daddy looked over at her and sort of scowled and said, "Oh, hush, Mamma."

17

Mr. Marcus

and the Overhead Bridge

When I heard the other day that Mr. Marcus Bascomb had killed himself by jumping off the overhead bridge in Woodville, it set me to thinking about all sorts of things that hadn't crossed my mind in a long time, I've been gone from there so long. And yet I always feel, wherever I go, that Woodville is the largest part of me and that I still see things through Woodville eyes. So when I heard about Mr. Marcus, it brought back a lot of things from the past that I hadn't really forgotten but had just pushed into the back of my mind.

Woodville was right on the main line of the L. & N. Railroad, but, of course, the fast trains didn't stop there. You always had to get off at Marion at some uncomfortable hour of the night and be met. But at least in Woodville the L. & N. didn't run right through the middle of the town and have to have all sorts of grade crossings and warning signals, the way it is in so many small towns. People used to say that Woodville wasn't anything but ridges and ravines, and in the old days the railroad had evidently been put through to make the most use of the ravines. It ran right through the town between the ridges in a deep cut, and the only way you ever saw the track was to look down whenever you were crossing the overhead bridge. I don't know why they called it that except that it was overhead of the railroad; but, when I was a little boy, I didn't like to walk across it because you could look over the railing and see the track nearly a hundred feet below and it always made me shiver. I didn't even like to watch the trains from there—as fond as I was of them.

But the overhead bridge was a sort of central fact about Woodville. No other town in that part of the world had anything like it, and it was the only way you could get from one side of town to the other. Somehow you felt that if anything ever happened to it, Woodville might just dissolve. Even when I was grown up and had lived in several different parts of the country, the overhead bridge was always one of the things I remembered right off when I thought about Woodville.

And one thing that always came up in your mind when you thought of the overhead bridge was the people that had jumped off it. I myself remember two or three prominent men around town who did it when I was growing up, and there were several Negroes who had, too. (Somebody even made a joke about the white people and the Negroes always jumping off different sides.) Most of them were killed instantly, and none of the others lived more than a few hours. I used to wonder why they had all chosen that particular way to kill themselves, and I never came to much conclusion about it except that they might have been afraid of losing their nerve and, certainly, jumping off the overhead bridge wasn't something you could change your mind about once you had started it. But I never worried much about that "side" of the overhead bridge. The bridge was just there, and you just had to take it as it was. If people wanted to jump off it, there wasn't much of anything you could do about it. And I think that was the way most of Woodville felt about it. When anybody did jump off it, they would usually just shake their heads and say, "Poor fellow, if that's the way he felt, he's better off out of his misery."

But back to Mr. Marcus Bascomb. Mr. Marcus came from one of the oldest families in town, and they really did live in a "white-columned Southern mansion," like it always says in the travel folders. And when you thought about what all he had done in his life, it sounded just like a novel in one of the women's magazines. To start with, Mr. Marcus had had all sorts of "advantages." Old Mr. Bascomb had sent him up North to Harvard to school; and after he had graduated from there, he sent him over to England to Oxford. Mr. Marcus was what everybody called "naturally studious," and old Mr. Bascomb had told somebody once that Mr.

Marcus didn't seem to be fit for anything except to go to school and he didn't know what else to do with him. But he was terribly proud of him all the same.

While Mr. Marcus was at Oxford, the First World War broke out, and he went right off to fight in France with the British Army and just missed getting the Victoria Cross (because he was an American, people said). And after the war, he decided to stay on and live in Paris, where he knew a lot of writers and artists. Mr. Marcus never did produce much of anything in the way of art himself, but he must have liked to be around where it was always going on, and he liked to travel. And now you heard he was in Spain or Italy or somewhere else over there.

But from time to time he would come back to Woodville—always unexpectedly—and see his family and all the people he had grown up with. And he would sit out in the courthouse yard and very skillfully "draw out" some of the old "characters" who sat there every day under the shade of the big oak trees when it was summer; one or two people said he wasn't doing anything but just loading up on Woodville tales to take back to Europe with him. But when I was growing up, I thought Mr. Marcus was the most "romantic" figure that ever was—certainly around Woodville: a sort of cross between Rupert Brooke and Robinson's Richard Cory, who "glittered when he walked." He was tall and slim, with piercing blue eyes and the most beautiful smile I've ever seen on a man. He was every inch the "Southern gentleman" in his manners, and he hadn't ever lost his accent either. Every now and then somebody who knew something about things would ask him what he was doing over there in Europe and who all he knew of the writers and artists. And Mr. Marcus would laugh and say he was just a "booster," which was a term around Woodville for anybody that never did much of anything but was always on hand whenever there was any excitement. But once in a while he would talk about some of his European friends—all of them well known or well born—but he was always very modest about it. He never was what we now call a name-dropper.

But after Mr. Marcus had been around town a month or so, he would all of a sudden pick up and go running off back to Europe. Some people said that Mr. Marcus had married a wife of the wrong sort over in France during the war and was ashamed to bring her home, that was why he was so mysterious about it all. And I know it used to worry the Bascombs a lot because they never knew where to write him or where he might be heard from next.

Of course, a lot of people said Mr. Marcus wasn't doing anything but just trying to spend all the money his father had left him and was probably carrying on all sorts of stylish wickedness over there. But Cousin Rosa Moss said that wasn't so at all. She said, "There never was a sweeter or more lovable child than Marcus Bascomb. I ought to know because I taught him both in the first grade and in the Baptist Sunday School. But the Bascombs always were a curious lot, and I don't think Marcus has ever been really happy. Don't ask me why; I'm sure all these highfalutin psychologists and things would have a field day with him. But I think that, for some reason, Marcus has always been afraid to let himself get mixed up in anything enough to love some particular person or some particular place, and you certainly do have to let yourself get mixed up in things when you do that. And that's why I think he keeps wandering around from one place to another so much. But finally he's bound to run out of places to go, and then I think he'll come right back here to Woodville for good. Anybody that was born and raised in Woodville is mixed up in it forever whether he likes it or not. One thing's certain: Woodville will be right here waiting for him when he does get ready to come back."

When I heard Cousin Rosa say that, I was still in my teens, and it all sounded like a lot of foolishness to me. How could anybody that had lived the glamorous life that Mr. Marcus had lived ever come back to Woodville to stay? I couldn't wait to get away from it myself—with all the people there who knew more about your business than you did yourself and were only too glad to tell you so. And I was sure that Mr. Marcus had more sense than to deliberately come back to Woodville to live.

Well, I went off to college, and after that I went up North to live. So I never did see much of Mr. Marcus any more because we were hardly ever in Woodville at the same time. And besides, after I had seen a few sights in far-off places and had a few adventures myself, I didn't know that Mr. Marcus had any special monopoly on romance any more. The last time I had seen him he had gotten quite gray.

But then just the other day I got a letter from my mother, telling me, among other things, that Mr. Marcus had come back to town very suddenly one night—nobody knew where from—and jumped off the overhead bridge. Nobody even knew he was in town until the section gang found his body on the track the next morning.

I hadn't thought about Mr. Marcus in a long time, but for the last two or three days I haven't been able to get him out of my mind. And I've thought a lot about what I heard Cousin Rosa say that time. And I've wondered whether Mr. Marcus had known all along that, when he finally ran out of places to go, Woodville— and the overhead bridge—would be right there waiting for him.

18

By Thy Good Pleasure

I wasn't as shocked as I might have been when Daddy died because he had had a little spell with his heart several years before—the last year I was in high school. Now I was off at college, majoring in English; it was Easter vacation and I was home. Daddy and I had gone to Memphis the day before, and, when I got tired on the way home, he even took the wheel and drove for a while.

He and Mamma and I were all at the breakfast table, and we were talking about whether Miss Annie Coleman that we had seen in Memphis the day before was any kin to somebody out in the Maple Grove community. I got up to get the coffee off the stove, and suddenly there was a crash behind me and Mamma screamed. Daddy was stretched out on the floor with his coffee cup beside him; and she was bending over him, holding his head and crying, "Daddy, oh, Daddy, speak to us. What *is* the matter?"

At first I was almost too stunned to move, but then I ran to the telephone and called Dr. Wilson that lived up on the corner and asked him to come right down. But when I got back to the kitchen, Mamma said, "Oh, I think he's gone." And I said, "Oh, no, he just can't be." And yet I think I knew he was. He was right there, and any minute he might raise up and say he had been fooling. He used to scare me by playing possum like that when I was little. But he just lay there now, just like a stone. I ran back to the telephone and called Uncle Buford down at Drake Brothers, and by that time Dr. Wilson was coming in the front door.

He bent down over Daddy and listened to him, and then he looked at Mamma and me and said, "He's had a coronary." Then he gave him a shot, but I think he knew right then it wasn't any use. By the time Uncle Buford got there, Dr. Wilson said Daddy was gone. Uncle Buford went and started calling up the neighbors and the rest of the family, and before you knew it, they were all coming in the house. Mamma was just dazed, but as every new one would come in, she would hug them and say, "Oh, I wish we could have all gone together, but that wouldn't have been fair to Robert." But she hardly knew who she was talking to or what she was saying.

I was standing there with everything going on all around me, not really feeling anything. Ever since I had been little I had dreaded the day when Mamma and Daddy would die; now that it was really happening, I didn't seem to be able to take it in. I knew I ought to be crying or something, and yet I just couldn't. It was like I was finally acting out a part I had been preparing for for a long time, and I was as calm as I had ever been in my life.

Finally, they got me to take Mamma into her room while Mr. Purdy, the undertaker, came for Daddy. I sat there beside her not knowing what to say. We had always been so close and knew each other so terribly well that now there wasn't anything to do except hold her tight and tell her Daddy wouldn't have wanted to go any other way. Dr. Wilson said he probably never knew what happened; it was that quick. Mrs. Henry from next door came in and got Daddy's clothes that he had worn the day before and put them out of the way. And then people began to come in with flowers and food and what-all until I thought I just couldn't say thank you another time. But still I couldn't *feel* anything. Daddy was gone, and I didn't feel anything. What was wrong with me?

When it came time to talk about the arrangements, which everybody in Woodville always called the funeral and burial, Mamma said she wanted Daddy brought back home to lie in state. But Uncle Buford and I talked her out of it because we thought it would be so hard on her. She kept saying, over and over, "But Daddy always said he wanted to be brought back home." But we told her it would be the best thing to leave him at the funeral home. Then when we decided to have the funeral the next morning at ten o'clock, she said, "Don't you think that's a little soon? Do you think Daddy would feel we weren't doing right by him?" But I said no, Daddy never had liked a lot of going-on at funerals: he always thought the main thing was to *love* people while they were still with you. And when Brother Parks, the preacher, came around, I told him we didn't want anything in the service but the Methodist ritual: Daddy had always said that was good enough for anybody.

The day went on with more and more people coming in and talking and more and more flowers arriving. Brother Harris, a Methodist preacher from out at Haley's Switch that Daddy had always thought a lot of, came in and offered to pray with us; but, while he was thanking God for Daddy's life and everything, I was just standing there thinking: my Daddy is dead, he really is, and I don't feel *anything*, it's just like it was somebody else. There wasn't anybody could tell us anything about Daddy we didn't know; we knew he was the kindest man in the world and the most tenderhearted. One man did come up and say, "You know, if there ever was a man that had realized most of his ambitions, it was your Daddy. Because he lived to see you get all the education he had never had and wanted you to have, and he saw you well on the way to getting whatever you wanted in life." (I remembered when he had had that first spell with his heart and the doctor was bending over him giving him one shot after another. And Daddy whispered, "I don't want to go now, but if I do, it's all right. I've made enough money to get my boy through school like I promised him.") And now Daddy's love was right there all around me in the people he had loved and had loved him in return, and yet somehow I still felt like an outsider.

Later, when we went up to the funeral home to see Daddy and all the flowers, it made me feel even worse. There he was stretched out in a casket in his Sunday suit and the tie I had given him for his birthday the month before and he had never worn, but I couldn't feel close to him there. He looked too made-up and prim, and Daddy never had been that way in his life. And all those flowers from the florists' made me feel just like when I was a little boy; they made me sick at my stomach. And people came in to talk, and I talked to them like Daddy might not even be lying there.

The next morning the sun was shining, and all the bridal wreath and redbuds and dogwoods were drenched in light. But it was still kind of chilly, like it can be in April. I got dressed for the funeral, just like I was going to church on Sunday; after a while all the family started coming in, and we were ready to go. When we got to the church, the casket was already there in front of the pulpit, covered with red and white carnations. Mamma was holding on to me as tight as she could, but I was hardly paying any attention to her. I was thinking how terrible it was that Daddy was dead right there in that casket and I still somehow didn't feel anything about losing him.

Then the quartet got up to sing and started in on "Rock of Ages," and I remembered all of a sudden that it was Good Friday. People always sang "Rock of Ages" on Good Friday. My "literary" friends at school would enjoy that, I thought: my father was buried on Good Friday. All sorts of parallels and ironies started coming into my mind, and I could think about them just as calmly and analytically as you please. And then the quartet sang "Nearer, my God, to Thee." And I remembered that that was what they had played when the *Titanic* went down. No, somebody had come along and shown, by precise documentation, that they had played something else. I wasn't surprised; nothing like that surprised me any more. Somebody always came along and disproved all the things that had meant something; I was expecting any day to have somebody come out and prove, beyond peradventure of doubt, that Mary Tudor had never burned a single Protestant.

When the service was over, we filed out behind the casket while the organist played "Now the Day Is Over." There was a bad minute there at the door when I thought the pallbearers might drop the casket getting it off the trolley it had been resting on to take it out to the hearse. I thought how terrible it would have been to drop Daddy like that, and yet I wasn't horrified or anything. It would just have been ironic, that's all.

I had asked Mamma if she wanted to bury Daddy down at Mr. Moriah Cemetery out from Barfield, where most of the Drakes were buried. But she said she wouldn't be able to get down there very often and would rather bury him down at Oakwood Cemetery in Woodville. So that was where we were going, and Daddy was going to be buried alongside Mamma's parents, Grandma and Grandpa Wood that had died before I was born. And there would be a space left for Mamma and one for me. When I was telling Mr. Purdy what we wanted to do, I couldn't even think very much about that place just sitting there, waiting for me. Why get all upset about it? You knew you had to die someday, and that was that.

Oakwood was down by the canning factory, and the railroad ran right along one side of it. And as we got out of the car, a long old freight train zoomed by behind a triple diesel unit. And then all of a sudden right there while Brother Parks was pronouncing the benediction, I began to think about how I had always liked trains, ever since I was little, and how Daddy used to take me down to the station every Sunday between Sunday School and church so I could see the eleven o'clock passenger train from Memphis come by. Now there weren't any big old black steam engines chugging through any more; there were just diesels, throbbing powerfully in a cool, restrained sort of way. It was strange that that was what I should be thinking about right there when we were burying Daddy.

When we got home from the cemetery, nearly everybody had left except the family, who were all going to stay for dinner. Everybody was talking about how pretty the flowers had been and how nice the music was when Lina Davis, my cousin from over at Monroeville, spoke up and said, "You know, I was just looking around this morning when we were going in the church. And you know, we just don't have much family any more." And it was so: Uncle Jim, Lina's father, had died suddenly a few years before, just like Daddy. And last fall Uncle Wesley down at Barfield had died of cancer. (Mamma wrote me—I was off at school—that it like to have killed Daddy to see him suffer so.) I wondered who would be the next of the uncles, or whether it would be one of us younger ones— like my cousin Stuart that I adored that was killed in the war. I thought about all the other funerals in the family—Uncle Wesley's and Stuart's and Aunt Janie's, Uncle Buford's first wife that almost sang her heart out in the Methodist Choir and all over the county, really almost loved her life away, and I wondered when there would be another one.

Finally, the family began to go; even Uncle Buford and dear, fine Susan that he married a few years after Aunt Janie died, went home. There was nobody there now but Mamma and me. I told Mamma to go lie down: she needed to rest. And, for a wonder, she was too tired to put up much of a struggle. I went in and took off my Sunday suit and put on some everyday clothes and went out and sat on the back steps.

Everywhere the afternoon sun was streaming down into the back yard: through the big pecan trees that Uncle Tom Henry next door had planted nearly seventy-five years ago and through Grandma Wood's fig bushes that were now as tall as the house. There were the little peach trees that Daddy had planted as soon as he was able after his illness two years ago, and now they were blooming. Everything was terribly, overwhelmingly alive. And Daddy was dead. He would never see those peach trees again.

All of a sudden, I bent over and cried; I wasn't even sure what I was crying about. I wasn't exactly thinking about Daddy so much as I was about his *love*, how there just wasn't a selfish bone in his body, and how he couldn't bear for anybody else to be selfish. I never had known anybody else but Daddy that could *completely* forgive people when they mistreated him, sometimes his own flesh and blood. And I remembered how he wasn't ashamed to cry when anybody he loved was sick or in trouble and needed him. Daddy was maybe very eighteenth-century in that way; he wasn't afraid of tears, and I guessed maybe it was because he wasn't afraid of love. Because you had to love in order to cry, and most people now were really afraid of love. Maybe, in a way, that's what I was crying about—not Daddy so much as his love. That was the only love I had ever known that had accepted me fully, completely, and without asking any questions; I knew that now. That was what I was really crying about. And why was it always when you let yourself love somebody in return, something always happened? Look at Aunt Janie and Stuart and Mrs. Edney, my high school English teacher that taught me poetry was maybe just another way of looking at God—people that weren't afraid of love—and all of them gone. And now Daddy. I shuddered with crying. I couldn't take any more; I wouldn't *let* myself love anybody else, ever again.

Then I thought once more about it being Good Friday. That was what it meant to love: Good Friday and being crucified. I knew my "literary" friends would say I was being obvious, but I just had to think about it that way. There was certainly enough *irony* and *tension* and *paradox* there to choke the biggest literary critic in the business. But it was true. When you loved, you had to take a risk, and when you took a risk, that meant you might lose. And yet you had to keep on taking that risk. Daddy had always done that, and I knew that I had to keep trying to do it too, even if it killed me. That was ironic; that's exactly what it *would* do. But it was so hard to keep on loving and losing; it was so hard to keep on dying. You got so tired of it all.

And then, for no reason at all, I began thinking about Louella, my old colored nurse, and the first song she ever taught me; it was "Amazing Grace." And I remembered one verse that went

> Thro' many dangers, toils and snares,
> I have already come;
> 'Tis grace hath bro't me safe thus far,
> And grace will lead me home.

And then I remembered another hymn I used to like when I was little and went to church with Mamma and Daddy and made out like I was playing the organ on the back of the pew in front of me: "Come, Thou Fount of Every Blessing." There was one verse that used to fascinate me because I didn't know what it meant about raising your Ebenezer. It started off

> Here I raise mine Ebenezer;
> Hither by Thy help I'm come;
> And I hope, by Thy good pleasure,
> Safely to arrive at home.

That was it. You had to keep on loving and giving up and then loving again. Not just because it was that way and you had to make the best of it, but because that was the only way, the only way to get *home.* And home was where you belonged—with Aunt Janie and Stuart and Mrs. Edney and Daddy and, yes, God. Even Woodville was just a temporary sort of home. Oh, it was terribly, terribly hard; and it might even really kill you. But there was God, whether you really believed in Him or not, always ready to reach out for you and bring you finally to Himself, not for any *reason,* but simply because it was His good pleasure. He knew what it was like to love, and so He knew what it was like to die. Maybe you really couldn't have one without the other. But what was really important was that it *was* His good pleasure for you finally to come home.

I had stopped crying now, but I sat there thinking about it all for a long time. And then I got up and went back in the house.

About the Author

Robert Drake was born (1930) and grew up in Ripley, Tennessee, the county seat of Lauderdale County and fifty miles north of Memphis. He was educated at Vanderbilt, where he worked under Donald Davidson, and at Yale, where Frederick A. Pottle supervised his doctoral dissertation. He has taught at the University of Michigan, Northwestern, and the University of Texas at Austin, and now teaches at the University of Tennessee, Knoxville, where he has been since 1965.

Amazing Grace was his first book, and since it appeared he has published three other collections of stories, a family memoir, and many articles and reviews in the learned and other journals.